HER FEARLESS WARRIOR

OMEGA SKY
BOOK 4

CAITLYN O'LEARY

To my sister Molly, who always amazes me. I love you to the moon and back, little sister.

SYNOPSIS

Finding Them? Simple.
Getting Them Out Alive? Now That Will Take a Minute.

Lincoln Hart's Navy SEAL team is sent to Syria to rescue a team of Americans who have been captured. When he realizes their interpreter, Leila Cloud is one of the people who has been kidnapped, all bets are off. He's been dreaming about her for months.

With their protective detail dead, Leila was determined to keep her small group unhurt and alive. Can she do this without making herself a target of their brutal captors?

Linc knows that finding the group of American's will be the simple part of the mission. Getting them out alive will be next to impossible.

PROLOGUE

Seven-year-old Lincoln Edison turned up the volume on his iPod as high as it would go and winced as Nickelback's lead singer tried to blow out his eardrums. He would do anything to block out the sounds from down the hall.

Despite Chad Kroeger's best attempts, Linc couldn't block out his mother's scream. Only one scream. Those were the worst. He grabbed his pencil so tight it broke. If his mom wasn't screaming, it meant that Dad was choking her or she'd passed out.

Or was this the time that Dad would finally kill Mom?

Ick churned through his stomach and he felt like he was going to throw up. He could hear them in their bedroom, so he snuck downstairs to the kitchen. He was barefoot, so he didn't make any noise. He'd learned how to be quiet when you're barefoot from that movie—he was pretty sure it was E.T. When he got to the kitchen, he reached up real high to get the phone off the hook from the wall.

He carefully dialed 911.

"Nine-one-one, what's your emergency?"

That lady was really loud. Linc pushed the receiver to his chest to make sure her voice couldn't be heard. He pulled the long cord so that he could move around the counter and scrunch down real small into the corner of the cupboards.

"You need to be quiet," he whispered to the lady.

"Okay. Can you tell me what your emergency is?"

"I think he's going to kill her this time." Linc choked back a sob.

"Are you someplace safe?"

"Yeah, I'm hiding in the kitchen."

"That's good. Now tell me your address."

Linc did. He had it memorized. "Is a policeman going to come?"

"Yes, honey. A police officer is going to come."

"Okay."

"Tell me your name."

"I've got to go back to my room. If he finds me here, I'll get it."

He got up from the corner and started to walk around the counter to hang up the phone.

"I need your name," she said louder.

She wasn't supposed to talk loud. Linc had already told her.

He reached up on his tiptoes and hung up the phone. He listened carefully and heard a shout, then a soft scream. That was another thing he hated, when Mom couldn't scream anymore. It meant that everything was getting worse.

He carefully made it back up to his room, making sure to close his door as quietly as he could. Then he went to his window and waited. It seemed like forever for the police car to drive up to the curb. They didn't have their lights flashing or their siren going, and he didn't understand why not. Two men got out of their car and knocked on the front door.

All the sound in his parents' bedroom stopped.

Then he heard his dad's shoes stomping down the hall, and Linc's door slammed open. "It was you!" his dad hissed.

His dad's eyes glowed as he towered over him. Then he did something he'd never done before. He hit Linc. He punched Linc in the stomach so hard that he landed against his bed. "You called them, didn't you, boy?"

Linc couldn't pull in air. He saw his mom behind his dad. She looked like she always did, scared and hunched over. That's because his dad was always sure not to hit anyplace that people could see.

"Because of you, you little shit, I'm going to have to go deal with them. When I come back, I'm going to come deal with you. In the meantime, you stay here and keep your trap closed. You got it?"

Linc nodded. He didn't know what else to do.

His dad gave him a funny look. And he strode further into the bedroom and picked Linc up by his Star War pajamas. "You know, I don't think you've got it." Linc looked up at eyes identical to his own. "If you make one peep, you do one little thing that brings attention to you, I will knock her into next Sunday," he said as he pointed to Linc's mom. "She's my wife. You're my kid. You both are my property. I can do whatever the fuck I want to each of you. You got that?"

Linc's father dropped him onto the floor, where he curled up into the fetal position, trying to ease the pain in his stomach.

"Come on, Connie. You better tell them nothing is going on. I want to see you smile, otherwise I'll start in on him." Following Linc's mom out, his dad shut his bedroom door.

Linc could hear them going down the stairs and then the front door opened. He dragged himself to his bedroom window so he could see and hear what was said. He opened the window just a little bit.

"Hello. What can I do for you?" his mother asked.

"We got a report of a domestic disturbance."

Linc looked at the two men on the porch. They were both bigger than his dad. They could make him stop hitting his mom.

"Are you sure you have the right house?" his mom asked. "My husband and I were just watching TV."

"May we talk to your husband?"

"Hold on and I'll get him."

She shut the door.

"Did you see the way she winced when she turned to close the door? I think she might have a broken rib," the tall policeman said.

"I don't know. She seems fine to me."

The door opened again. "Hi, I'm Bill Edison. My wife tells me you got a report of a domestic disturbance? Would you like to come in? I think there must be some kind of mistake."

"Bill's right. We weren't even playing the TV loud, so I don't understand."

"Do you have any children? They said that they thought it was a child who made the call," the tall policeman said.

"Yes, we have one son, Lincoln. He's seven years old," his mother answered.

"But he's sleeping over at a friend's house tonight. So, he couldn't have made any call. If he ever did that, we'd have to ground him for calling the police when there wasn't anything wrong."

"Therefore, we can't talk to your son?"

"If you want to go all the way over to Englewood. That's where the sleepover is happening." His dad laughed.

"BILL, would you mind coming out here and answering a few questions while my partner, Officer Gilbert, goes in and talks to your wife?"

"That would be just fine."

Linc could stand up now. He still couldn't take a full breath. He pulled up his pajama top and pressed his hand against the spot where his dad's fist had hit him. It felt really warm, and it hurt when he pressed on it. But Linc refused to cry. He hardly ever saw his mom cry, so he wouldn't cry.

He went to his bedroom door and slid it open just enough so he could slip out. He wanted to hear what his mom said to the tall policeman.

"Are there any firearms in the house, Mrs. Edison?"

"Only one gun. But Bill keeps it in a safe."

"Are you sure? Are you sure it's in a safe?"

"I'm positive. Bill keeps it for protection. Only his or my thumbprint can open the safe in case of an emergency."

The policeman sighed.

"Has your husband ever hit you, Mrs. Edison?"

"Never. No matter how mad he's gotten, he has never hit me," she lied.

"I noticed that you're walking slowly, and you're favoring your right side. Did you injure yourself?"

Please tell him, Mom. Please tell him. Please tell him.

"I worked out too hard yesterday during my exercise class at the gym. It usually takes me a day or two to recover."

Linc hit the stair railing in frustration.

"Ma'am, is somebody else in the house? What made that sound?"

"It's just our dog. He's afraid of strangers, so he hides upstairs whenever somebody new comes over."

"Mrs. Edison, if your husband hurts you, we can help. Now is the time to tell us. We can protect you."

"I've read stories about what happens when the husband is taken away for the night. Then he makes bail, and he's angrier than ever. Why would a smart woman ever tell the police anything?"

"There are shelters that are totally private. You would be safe," the tall police officer said.

"Look around this house. Like I would ever subject my boy to a shelter. This is his home. It is my home. My husband is a good provider, and he has never hurt me."

"Mrs. Edison, I've been called out on almost one hundred of these kinds of cases. Ninety percent of them, the husband or boyfriend escalates, and the woman ends up in the hospital."

"I told you, my husband has never hurt me. Why won't you believe me?"

"And usually," the policeman continued, like she hadn't even said anything, "the husband or boyfriend will eventually start hitting the kids. Is that what you want for your son?"

His mom was crying now. "How many times do I have to tell you he's not violent?"

"Is that what you want me to write in your statement? He has never hurt you?"

"Yes, write that down. I'll sign it."

Linc felt a tear trickle down his cheek.

He went back to his bedroom. He put on his earphones and cranked up the music to its highest volume and went back to doing his math homework.

He'd finished his math assignment and took out his spelling homework. He knew some kids had their parents help them, but most of the time, his mother was too sick to help him. Linc knew what *too sick* meant. Why had his mother lied to the police?

He looked down and saw water on his paper. He scrubbed his face with the sleeve of his Star Wars pajamas and started concentrating on the words in front of him.

"You little shit!"

He was shoved so hard that he flew off his chair, and his headphones came off.

"It was you!" His father kicked him in his side. Linc cried out.

"Don't hurt him," his mother begged. She grabbed at his dad's arm and he wrenched away from her, causing her to stumble. As she gripped Linc's dad's arm, Linc saw his dad clench both of his hands into fists and he hit her so hard, in the face this time, that she fell down. Linc thought he'd killed her until she moaned.

Linc's dad kicked him really hard in his butt. "Get up," he yelled. "I'm not done with you."

Linc pushed up from the floor, listening to his mother's whimpers. When he was on his feet, his father grabbed his shoulders and shook him.

"I'm a good father to you. Do you hear me? I make sure you can live like a little fucking prince," he snarled.

Linc was dizzy and having trouble understanding what his dad was saying.

"Answer me. Do you hear me?"

"Yes." He somehow managed to get the word out.

"Yes!" His dad stopped shaking him, and continued to hold him with one hand, and with the other, backhanded him across the face. The world exploded in pain. He cried out.

"Shut up. Don't make a fucking sound. You take your punishment like a man."

"Bill, stop. He's just a little boy."

His dad dropped him, and Linc stared as his dad took three steps toward his mom and punched her in the stomach. She bent over, then he hit her with his other fist under her jaw. Her head snapped back and she hit the blue wall of his bedroom then slid down it. Her bathrobe split open so that her boobs were showing. Linc looked back at his dad.

"Stop hurting her," he shouted.

"You're right. I will. You still need to be taught a lesson. I think you need a bare-assed spanking. You wait right here." His father stalked out of his room, and Linc slumped to the floor. He needed to get to his mom. He crawled to her. He'd almost made it until his dad was back holding one of his belts.

He picked Linc up by the neck of his pajamas. Then his dad sat down on his twin bed with the Chewbacca bedspread, and he shoved Linc over his lap. He pulled down Linc's pajamas, then Linc heard the slap of the belt hitting flesh. For a brief moment, he wondered what had happened, then fire erupted on his butt and he screamed.

"I told you not to make a sound. If you do, I'll only beat you harder. Do you understand?"

Linc had no breath to say anything.

His dad gripped him by his hair and twisted his neck so their eyes met. "Do you understand?"

"Yes," Linc wheezed.

"That was one. You get ten. You'll end up bloody, but you deserve it for calling the cops. If you scream again, it'll be twenty."

Linc lost count of how many times his dad hit him. The pain was excruciating. He bit his bottom lip as hard as he could so he wouldn't make a sound. Then his dad whipped him on his thighs, and he screamed again.

"You were so close to the end of your punishment."

Another eruption of pain blasted through his entire body. Everything went red. He heard his mom screaming again.

She wasn't supposed to scream.

"Don't, Mom," he wheezed out the words.

"Mom, don't scream," he begged.

"Leave my baby alone!" It was his mom, but she sounded funny.

He toppled to the ground as his dad stood up.

"You wouldn't dare!" his father roared.

"I'm not kidding, Bill. Don't you dare touch him again."

Ahhhhhh, Linc moaned. The kick to his head made everything gray. He thought he heard more screaming and yelling, but he couldn't be sure.

"No, Mom." He thought he said the words, but he wasn't sure.

"Give me the gun, Connie. I'll stop."

"You'll never stop. That's what he said. You'll never stop."

"Just give me the fucking gun, you whore!"

Linc heard a loud explosion, then the world went black.

1

"No!" Elijah Hopkins roared.

Blood and bits sprayed Leila Cloud as Nottingham was shot in the head, his body hitting the rubble beside her.

"I'll go quiet—" Elijah didn't get to finish his sentence as Paul Unger was shot in the head. Now both bodyguards for their team were dead, killed in seconds.

Leila locked eyes with her boss. They'd worked together on and off for five years.

She knew him.

She knew him.

Yes, Elijah was angry, but for once she saw fear in his eyes.

"If you don't tell us what we want to know we'll start killing them, one by one. You understand?" The man holding Elijah with a gun pointed at his gut was speaking English. He didn't spare a glance for the two dead bodies at his feet, their brain matter mingling with some of the rubble that had once been a conference room in one of fifty interchangeable empty government buildings here in Damascus.

Leila listened carefully to the man. Based on his accent as he spoke English, it was clear that Arabic was his first language, but he wasn't from Damascus. She'd ponder this later. Now she needed to do something.

Anything.

"Why are you taking him? He's nobody. We all are." Leila manufactured tears as she spoke to the man. "Please, I'm begging you. We're scared. The room just exploded. We need help." At some point, they had set the room to blow, at least in the corners. Not enough to kill, just enough to shake them up.

She looked at the four men in front of her. The one holding Elijah clearly didn't care about her pleas. The two on either side of him had fanatical looks. They'd clearly drunk the Kool-Aid. But the young one, the one on the far right, he was buying into her act. The kid felt bad for her. She could use him. She memorized his face as she let a tear drip down her cheek.

"You Americans are so stupid," the leader sneered. He spit on the ground and shoved the pistol harder into Elijah's gut. Her boss groaned in pain. Yep, Leila wasn't the only one who could act. The leader turned and spoke in rapid Arabic to the man on his right. "Get their weapons." He tilted his chin to the two bodies on the ground.

The man nodded, then shoved both bodies over and reached inside their suit jackets and pulled their guns out of their holsters.

"Now, search the rest of them for weapons. Take away all of their electronics," the leader said in English. He pointed to his other man. "You help."

It took some time, but the two men confiscated all of

their laptops, and each one of them handed over their cell phones as a rifle was pointed at their heads. Then the two of them fell back in line next to their leader.

"Should we search the others?" one fanatic asked.

"They're nobody. Sheep. Don't bother, they won't have anything hidden," the leader laughed.

A heavy, short man named Robert Landry, who had been the bane of her existence, pushed past her so hard she almost lost her balance.

"If it's money you want, I can buy and sell that man a hundred times over," he said, pointing at Elijah. "Let me call the states and I can have a million dollars wired to whatever account you name. Then at least you can let me go." Robert's fawning tone wasn't an act, he was just that much of a bottom feeder. He only cared about his own ass.

What was more pathetic, he was a *cheap* lowlife. Leila knew how much money he had in his accounts, down to the last dollar. A million? He could pay ten million without batting an eye.

The stupid bastard!

"What's your name? How do I know you're telling me the truth?" the leader asked.

"Do an internet search. My name is Robert Landry. I own Landry Oil and Chemicals."

"I will," the leader said, giving Landry a considering look.

Did Landry have any sense at all?

Scratch that. Of course, he didn't. This was the man who inherited his father's and grandfather's company and was systematically running it into the ground. He was dumb as a bull in mating season.

"Meanwhile, Mr. Hopkins, we are going to have a long talk." The leader shoved Elijah toward what used to be a door but was now just an empty doorframe. They had kicked it in when the explosives went off.

"Don't do any—" Elijah started to say, then the leader pistol whipped him across the face. One of the two guards that Leila considered fanatical terrorists grabbed Elijah and shoved him upright so that he could continue to follow the leader.

"Stay and watch them," the leader growled out in Arabic to the youngest thug. "If any of them tries to escape, shoot them."

"Yes, Colonel Aydin." The young man stood up straight. "I will not fail you."

Leila watched as they practically dragged her boss across the rubble strewn on the top floor of the small building. They were bypassing the elevator and heading for the stairs. The explosion had been targeted to the conference room, nothing outside of their room had been destroyed. They'd known what they were doing. They hadn't wanted the people inside to die. Nope, just enough blast to make everyone inside duck for cover.

As Leila watched her boss stumbling in front of the leader, she hoped he was playing possum and was really okay, but that pistol had hit him hard.

"Please help us," Leila pleaded with the young guard, trying to suss out if he understood any English.

He turned around. "Silence, or you will be shot," he shouted in Arabic.

She had it. They were all speaking the Arabic language with a Mesopotamian accent. That was the accent used in Northeastern Syria, ISIS, and Al Qaeda territory. It didn't mean these assholes were necessarily terrorists, it could just as easily be Bashar al-Assad's goons. But then again, Assad wanted what they were supposedly selling, so he didn't have any motive to go after them.

Enough processing, time for more action.

"I must relieve myself. Don't make me debase myself in front of these men. I beg of you. Would you want your sister or your mother to squat so close to men?"

That should upset a good Islamic boy. He didn't flinch.

Good, he doesn't understand English.

"Please," she begged louder.

He walked over what was left of the conference room door's threshold and jabbed the muzzle of his automatic rifle into her gut. "Silence," he yelled in Arabic. He jabbed the muzzle again and again until she fell backwards onto her ass.

"Now wait a damned minute," Landry stepped forward. Faster than you could spit, the kid had a knife in his hand and he sliced it across Landry's fat belly.

And he was supposed to be the nice terrorist.

Landry screeched and jumped backward, holding his gut, but Leila didn't see any blood seeping through his fingers. The young man laughed. Then he put his forefinger to his lips. His meaning was clear. He wanted silence.

Leila tried to think. How many other terrorists were there? She didn't think it was just the four of them.

Why were northeastern Syrians here in Damascus? The only thing that made sense was that they were with ISIS or Al Qaeda, and they didn't want Assad to get any kind of advantage. How did they know that their tiny little delegation was here to broker a lucrative deal for al-Assad here in Syria? At least that was their cover story. Katherine Cole, with her hybrid soybean operation, and Landry with his oil and chemical business, were supposedly going to help bring American business to Syria, which would mean money. American business that would be outside the scope of USAID, so there would be profits that would line the pockets of Katherine and Landry and, especially al-Assad.

Even better, it would eventually mean other American investors. It was a perfect cover story that would keep that greedy fucking bastard al-Assad on their side. Nope, al-Assad wasn't behind this operation. He wouldn't want to bite the hand that could feed it.

But these guys? How did they know Elijah was really the big fish, and he was the one who was trying to meet with one of al-Assad's underlings who was willing to trade over five million dollars in diamonds to get four people out of prison?

There was a leak, and since al-Assad knew nothing yet, it had to be on the US side of things.

Goddammit!

"I need a doctor!" Landry bellowed. "I'm going to die! Your leader won't be happy if I died. He'll lose out on millions."

"So now it's millions, huh?" Felix Ratcliff moved forward and pushed Landry's hand out of the way. He tore his shirt farther apart and looked at the wound. "It's as deep as a paper cut. You're going to be fine." Felix looked over his shoulder at Leila. "No English? Are you sure?"

Leila nodded. "We need a diversion so that we can get to Nottingham and Unger's weapons."

"What are you talking about?" Landry demanded to know. "They took their weapons. Weren't you watching?"

Leila rolled her eyes at Felix, who gave the kind of sigh that only an old man who had seen everything could give.

"Landry, we need to check for their hidden weapons,"

Felix explained. Leila appreciated him stepping in. Right now, she didn't need to get into a dick measuring contest with Landry, she just needed results.

Landry frowned. "What are you talking about?"

"Robert, I need your help," Leila said in the most pleasant tone of voice she could muster. Hell, she sounded downright submissive!

Ick!

"What? We don't have much time. What do you need?" The man blustered.

Leila pushed out her boobs, what little she had. "I just know you could figure out a way to get that man's attention so Felix could look to see if the bodyguards were carrying any hidden weapons. You're the only one who could capture his attention. I just know it."

Katherine Cole made a sound behind them that sounded like she was choking. Leila knew she was trying not to laugh.

"Can you tell me the word for doctor in Arabic?" Landry asked. As the interpreter for the small delegation, Landry knew Leila would know the word.

Leila sounded out the Arabic word for doctor. After five tries, Landry still wasn't getting the correct pronunciation.

"Why don't you ask?" he wanted to know in frustration.

"Because we don't want any of them to realize she knows their language. She will be our ace in the hole," Katherine said. Katherine repeated the word for doctor in Arabic. She walked over to Landry and casually wiped her hands on his open wound, smearing her hands with his blood. "Come on, Robert. Let's go distract the boy. I might not have the femme fatale look like I did in my younger days, but I sure can play the mama card."

"But he's dangerous. He cut me."

God, please don't let the big bastard start whining.

Katherine yanked on the beefy man's arm and they moved forward, blocking the view of the two dead men. She started talking and Leila smiled as she saw that the older woman was definitely getting the young man's attention.

2

LEILA TOOK NOTTINGHAM AND FELIX TOOK UNGER. SHE rested her hand on Nottingham's chest and closed her eyes for a brief moment, praying that God would look out for these two brave men. Then she got to work. She pulled up both of Nottingham's pant legs. She found a Sig P365.

Score.

Come on, pal, what else have you got?

She did a thorough check of both arms and came up with nothing. There was nothing around his body except for an empty shoulder holster.

"Look on his belt buckle," Felix said. "He might have a knife."

She looked but saw nothing. Felix left Unger and came over to her and squatted over Nottingham. He turned the man's body onto his stomach and lifted his jacket. Same thing that Leila had done, but then Felix showed her the knife sheath that was hooked horizontally into the belt. He pulled a wicked-looking knife out of the sheath.

"You're good," Leila grinned.

"Lots of practice," Felix gave her a wan smile. He pulled the knife sheath off of Nottingham's body and connected it to his belt. "Unger had a Glock 43. What did you get?"

She looked up and saw that Katherine and Landry were still at it, then turned her attention back to Felix.

"Sig P365. Any preference?" she asked.

"No," Felix answered. "You?"

"I've trained more with the Glock," she admitted.

He handed the Glock and an extra magazine to her, and she handed over the Sig with the extra magazine.

They stood up and moved back to where the last two members of the delegation were standing. Sam Phelps looked shell-shocked and Annie Trent had stopped crying, so that was a plus.

Leila's head swung back to Landry, Katherine, and their captor, as the young man let loose a torrent of Arabic. Katherine was trying to diffuse the situation, but by the sounds of things, Landry had pissed the kid off. Leila might have asked for a diversion, but not fucking World War III.

Leila rushed up to where the arguing was going on. She understood what the kid was saying, and it wasn't good. He had his cell phone out and was planning to ask his leader if he had permission to kill one of the prisoners now.

Nope, not good at all.

Leila pushed her way between Landry and Katherine, then fell down at their feet, right in front of their captor. "Help," she said in Arabic. "Please." Another word in Arabic. She made sure that her pronunciation was terrible.

She grabbed her abdomen. "My baby." Another

phrase she mispronounced, but it was enough for the kid's eyes to widen.

She did not know if this ploy would work, but she prayed it would.

"Please help me," she said in English.

The kid put his cell phone back in his pants pocket. He looked frightened. He pointed his gun at Landry, then pointed to the back of the room, clearly telling him to go away and join the others. Landry ran faster than The Flash, his bloody gut wobbling all the way.

The kid bent down in front of Leila and reached out with his left hand, not quite touching her, but obviously freaked out.

It was the chance she needed. She grabbed that hand and yanked, rolling so that her legs could get into position to kick the kid's gut. In one smooth move, she yanked his arm that wasn't holding his weapon and pushed up on the kid's stomach so that he went up and over her head and landed on his back. Before he had a chance to do anything more than grunt in surprise, Felix was there to stab the knife into his jugular, spraying blood all over himself.

Annie shrieked softly.

"Really?" Leila shook her head. "I'm covered in blood."

"Did he yell for help?" Felix asked. "No, he didn't."

"We need a plan." Leila said grimly.

"What we need to do is to negotiate with the terrorists. That's what I do best," Landry blustered. He stepped over the third dead man in the hollowed-out board room. "That's the reason I was brought here. Let me take care of things. Leila, you need to come with me and translate."

She looked at him. Her job was to keep everybody in the dark. Nobody was supposed to know what the actual mission was. Supposedly, they were there to do business with al-Assad's government here in Syria so that their economy could be helped, thus helping thousands of displaced and starving nationals.

Yeah, like America would do this kind of business with al-Assad that would be lining his pockets. The US had their AID program that ensured the Syrian people directly got the food and medical care they needed, totally keeping al-Assad out of the loop. Leila was still amazed that Landry had bought into this bullshit story, but he had. She was pretty sure that Katherine saw through the bullshit, but she was on board because she and Elijah had a past together. Anyway, it was because of those two that it had been so easy for them to come to Damascus and do their actual business and that was to negotiate the release of four Americans who had been living through hell in Syrian prisons for what must seem like eternity.

Katherine had ripped down one of the curtains and had torn it up and was using it to help Felix wipe off the blood that had sprayed on him.

"Here, Leila, you need to clean up as well. Besides the blood…"

That was when she remembered that Nottingham had been shot right beside her, and she had been sprayed with… with…

Never mind. Put it away. Think about it some other time.

"Thanks, Katherine." Leila gratefully took the cloth and wiped up. She didn't look at what was coming off her face, hair, and neck. She didn't want to know.

"Now that you look more presentable, let's go."

Leila looked at Felix, who was checking out the dead man's AK-47. It's what she would do too, not trusting that it was in good working order. Felix was also grabbing all the ammunition he could from the dead man's body.

"I've got another knife. You want it, Leila?" Felix asked.

"Give it here," she said, holding out her hand.

"Are you crazy?" Landry said, looking at Felix. "Why would you give her a knife? Give it to me. Give me the rifle, too. Back home, I'm a hunter. Even been on safari twice. I know what I'm doing."

Felix continued to check the body for anything else that might be helpful. He pulled out the cellphone and tossed it to Leila. "Is it password-protected?" he asked.

Leila looked at the old-fashioned flip phone and smiled. She opened it and smiled grimly. "No password. There are even pictures beside the names. I'd say we hit pay dirt."

"Quit talking about the goddamned phone and give me the rifle. We need to show strength. I need the rifle to go down to those assholes and tell them who's in charge."

Leila looked over at Felix. He'd been a dark horse since their little group had shown up together in Germany. Elijah had clearly been their leader. He'd provided brief biographies of each player. Of course, Robert Landry had expanded his.

Pompous asshole.

Leila was the translator and a perpetual student. Supposedly, she knew Arabic and English and had been translating for over eight years.

Full stop.

But she was a lot more, and that was something Elijah would be counting on.

Katherine Cole was the C.E.O. of a company that bio-engineered soybeans, as well as working with emerging, (read: desperate), countries to produce nutrient-rich, easy-to-grow beans. Felix Ratcliff was supposedly representing the US department of foreign and affairs and trade. Elijah hadn't filled her in on Felix's background, but she'd bet her bottom dollar he was CIA. Leila's father was in the FBI. She'd been around enough agency men to sniff one out.

Annie Trent was Katherine's secretary, which was a goddamn shame. Talk about bringing a lamb to slaughter. Then there was Sam Phelps. At least he had a stint in the Marines twenty years ago, but he lost his leg. Not that anyone would really notice, but he was Robert Landry's number two, and could end up being a liability.

"Leila, get a move on. Felix, give me that rifle." Landry went to wrest it out of Felix's hands.

Not a good move.

Felix stood up. He wasn't as big as Landry. As a matter of fact, he was on the skinny side. He was pale and balding, with glasses. He looked like an accountant. But he had his suit jacket off now, and his sleeves rolled up. Leila couldn't help but notice Felix's muscled forearms. Any woman would. Landry didn't. At least not until Felix easily pulled back the AK-47, not releasing it to Landry.

"I said give it to me."

"You ever shot one of these?" Felix asked in a mild voice.

"No, but I've shot plenty of hunting rifles. This can't be much different. Now give it over. I'll get Elijah back, and we'll get the hell out of here and report this shit at the American Embassy."

"Robert, America doesn't have an embassy here in Syria," Leila told him.

"What in the hell are you talking about? Of course, they do," he blustered. "The United States has an embassy in all countries."

Leila pressed her fingers against the bridge of her nose.

"No, they don't. We oppose the al-Assad regime, so we don't support him by having an embassy. That's why we're here having this meeting undercover. You know that, you were briefed."

"I knew we were doing this secretly. We're here to help Syria get back on its feet by providing businesses and food. No one explained we didn't have an embassy."

"Robert, it was explained to us in our meetings back in D.C.," Katherine spoke up. "Elijah and the Secretary of State told us that we needed to do this undercover and we would do this without the formal backing of the United States. You agreed to this, just like I did. We wanted to help."

"No, I wanted to make money," Landry protested. "This is the first opportunity my company has in getting a foothold in Eastern Europe. The E.U. doesn't want to do business with me, but al-Assad will."

Leila gave Katherine the side-eye. Katherine opened her mouth to explain the situation again. "Save your breath, Katherine," Felix said with a grimace. "You're never going to convince him."

Katherine sighed. "You're right."

"Now give me the rifle."

"You're not going anywhere," Leila stated. "With Elijah gone, I'm in charge, and we sure as hell aren't going to go confront those bastards. We have no idea how many we're dealing with, now do we?"

"No," Landry admitted.

"If you and I were to go down there half-cocked, then they could just as easily come up here and start killing whomever we leave behind. Are you willing to risk that?"

"Well, what else do you suggest, little Miss I'm-in-Charge?"

"I'm going to call in our situation to the Captain of the USS Fielding, who is currently doing maneuvers off the coast of Syria, and explain our situation."

"And then what?"

"We position ourselves at the entrance to the stairs and the elevators with the weapons we have and attempt to take someone alive so we can question them," Felix answered.

Leila reached under her blazer, then pulled out a state-of-the-art cell phone from the waistband of her slacks. "This phone is secure," she said to the crowd.

Captain Evers answered on the first ring.

"Leila. What's your problem?"

"Captain, we're in an empty government building in downtown Damascus. Either ISIS or Al Qaeda have us. They took Elijah for questioning. We don't know the total count of the terrorists. At this point, we can only be sure of three. We have some weapons and a plan to defend ourselves, but unknown if we can escape."

"Address of building?"

She provided it.

"Are you planning on rescuing Elijah?"

"Our plan is fluid. Our two bodyguards have been killed. I've got six civilians with me." She looked up at Felix. He held up his hand and held out five fingers. "Scratch, that Captain, I have five civilians and one other operative."

"Do what you have to do. Just keep me informed. I might have a plan I can put in place. I'll call."

"Much appreciated."

The line went dead.

She turned her attention to the group. "Who are you?" Landry demanded to know. "FBI? CIA? Military?"

"I used to work for the CIA. Now I'm going to school in Turkey to get another master's degree and support myself as a translator."

"And you?" Landry asked Felix.

"I freelance. Spent some time in the Army. Now I work for myself. I really like my boss."

"So, you're an asshole," Landry said with derision.

"You're really a piece of work, aren't you?" Felix rolled his eyes.

Leila and pretty much everybody else did what they could not to laugh. After that, Leila felt herself relaxing for the first time since the room exploded and Elijah had been taken.

"We have two pistols and a rifle. Sam, you were in the Marines. Are you still good with a pistol?" Leila asked.

"Give it to Landry. He won't be able to do anything with a knife. I will." Sam stepped up to Felix and held out his hand for the bloody knife.

"How good are you?" Leila asked.

"Good," Sam answered succinctly.

She handed over the sheath and knife she'd pulled off Nottingham and handed that over, too. Then she gave the PS-365 to Landry. "Make every shot count. There's only one extra magazine."

"So, how should we do this? Two at the stairs and two at the elevators?" she asked.

"I thought you were in charge," Landry said sarcastically.

"The elevators could hold more men at once. The rifle should be positioned there. The stairs have a narrower point of entry. A knife and a gun there," Felix said. "Leila, any preference?"

"I'll leave that to Sam."

"Leila, you're with me at the stairs," Sam said.

"Landry, you're with me at the elevators," Felix said. "Since there are two, we'll see which ones are coming up if we watch five feet in front of them. We can be prepared. I doubt that they'll be bringing Elijah back up. Leila, are we sure that there aren't going to be any civilians in this building?"

"This building has been unoccupied for a year, but there is always a chance our intel is wrong. The electricity is on, and the conference room table didn't have dust on it, so it's being cleaned. I think they have a cleaning crew, so you need to be on the lookout for that. They would come up in the elevators."

"Good call." Felix nodded. "Landry, got that?"

Landry nodded.

Leila looked over at Sam. "Sam, we can pretty much assume people coming up the stairs will be bad guys. Any shots fired would be at our targets. Remember, we need to take at least one alive."

"You're with me, Leila," Sam said again.

Leila nodded. She sure as hell hoped that Landry didn't end up killing any civilians.

"What should we do?" Katherine asked.

Leila handed over her secure cell phone. "I need you to monitor this. You know the situation; explain who you are, and mention mine and Elijah's names. They'll ask you more identifying questions. Just answer them."

"Got it."

"Do your best to memorize whatever they say."

"I still have my notebook and pen," Annie said as she

held them up. "I'm one of those people who still knows shorthand." She gave Leila a tentative smile.

"That's great, Annie. Get as much information as you can."

Leila turned to the rest of the crew. "Okay, men, let's take our positions."

3

—————

ALL FOUR OF THEM WERE IN A RESTING POSE. THEY'D BEEN like that for over two hours. Landry, of course, had not shut up. Poor Felix had to listen to his incessant bitching. At least she and Sam Phelps couldn't make out what he was saying.

"So, you were in the CIA?" Sam asked in the softest whisper.

They'd put a folded piece of paper in the lock plate, so that it was open just the tiniest bit. This would allow them to hear if anyone was coming up the steps. Leila would take any advantage she could get.

"Dad was FBI." Leila started to answer Sam's question. "I was studying languages and political science. I had a knack for it. My mom's parents live in Turkey, so I grew up speaking English, Turkish and Arabic."

"Arabic?"

"Made friends with my nanny's son when I was really young over in Turkey each summer to visit my grandparents. He didn't really speak much Turkish, so I worked to teach him, and he taught me Arabic. It helped that my nanny would speak to me in Arabic when my grandparents weren't around."

"What else?"

"Languages?"

Sam nodded.

Leila laughed. "Umm, French, Russian and Portuguese. It's funny, I can only speak Portuguese if I first translate my English to Russian then to Portuguese because I was in a Russian school where I learned Portuguese."

She saw the blank look on Sam's face and grinned. That was normal.

"My best is Turkish, English, Arabic, and Russian. I can speak, read, and write in those languages."

"You're shitting me."

"Nope."

"I've seen those alphabets. That's impressive."

"That's what the CIA thought. That's why they started trying to recruit me during my sophomore year in college. I refused until I got my degree. Then I went to work for them for two years before I bailed. What about you? What's your story? How'd you get hooked up with Landry?"

"I worked for his father. Now he was a good man. This idiot, not too much, but I promised Mitch I'd stand by Robert's side. This is the most fun I've had since Mitch died."

Leila shook her head. "Not sure you have your priorities straight, Sam."

"You sound like my three ex-wives."

"Three, huh?" Leila said with a grin. "Think you might want to ponder on the fact that all three said the same thing?"

"Nah, don't believe in introspection. Gives me indigestion."

Leila shrugged.

Live and let live.

"But you're good with knives?" she asked.

"Abso-fucking-lutely."

"Then you're a good man in my book."

They spent another half hour waiting and blocking out the sound of Landry gassing on. Poor Felix.

Leila and Sam jolted at the same moment. They looked at one another.

"Here that?" Sam asked.

Leila nodded. "How many do you think?"

"Do you hear them talking?

Leila nodded. She could hear three distinct voices. She held up three fingers. Sam nodded. They sounded like they were still two flights down. Leila carefully pulled the paper from the lock plate and softly closed the door. She winced at the click when the latch connected and the door properly closed. She put her ear to the door. She breathed a sigh of relief when she didn't hear any kind of change in their footsteps as they climbed the stairs.

She thought about calling Felix and Landry over, but there was still a slight possibility more terrorists might be coming up the elevator.

"Give me one of your knives," she said to Sam. "We need to be quiet. I don't want to shoot the gun if at all possible."

He nodded and handed over a knife. She hit the safety on the Glock and shoved it in the shoulder holster she'd pulled off Nottingham.

Sam took the right side of the door, Leila the left side.

The door opened. Leila heard four distinct voices; she

held up four fingers. Sam quickly nodded. They executed their plan perfectly. They let the first people go by as they remained flat against the walls on either side of the door. As the third and the fourth man exited, Leila took the third and Sam took the fourth. They yanked each man toward them, plunging their knives directly into their jugulars.

Leila didn't bother pulling the knife out. She had her hand at her holster, pulling out her Glock, and she killed the man who had his rifle up and was ready to shoot. Sam had tackled the second man who had come through the door.

The sound of bullets had Leila jerking. Where were they coming from? She looked over at the doorway and saw nothing.

"Die, you bastards, die!" she heard Landry yell.

Then there were more sounds of automatic fire, and it wasn't coming from just one rifle, it was coming from multiple rifles.

Landry screamed.

More gunfire.

Then she heard nothing but more bullets flying.

She turned her attention to Sam and the man he had tackled. The man was laughing. "You're going to die," he said in broken English.

Sam slit his throat, and Leila watched as a rifle butt crashed into Sam's jaw, sending him flying.

She looked up and saw the man who had seemed like the leader glaring down at her. He backhanded her and she sprawled backward, landing in a pool of blood.

"You're lucky I still need you, otherwise you would die right now. Of course, there are worse things than dying."

PETTY OFFICER, First Class, Lincoln Hart, the sniper for the Omega Sky SEAL team, looked at the faces of the people that they were expected to rescue.

Leila Cloud. Translator. Now there was a face he recognized.

He'd met her briefly on a mission they'd been on a year ago. She was a cool customer, and he'd liked what he'd seen. It wasn't just her physical attributes, it was her professionalism. The woman knew her stuff when it came to languages. Supposedly, she was a full-time student in Turkey getting another master's degree, this one in geology. Linc wasn't buying it. She didn't give off the vibe of a perpetual student. Especially geology. Now that he saw her on the screen with a high-ranking CIA official, he knew his suspicions were correct. Yeah, there were deeper depths to Ms. Cloud.

"Why are they in Syria?" his lieutenant, Kostya Barona, asked the man on the screen who was running the briefing. The team had had little info when they were deployed to the aircraft carrier, just that they were a contingency if things went wrong. They hadn't even been told which country they might be going into, Lebanon or Syria.

The man was Skyping from Langley, CIA headquarters. As usual, all of their team took what the CIA had to tell them with a grain of salt. Now not all CIA members, just the ones they didn't know.

"This was an off-the-books negotiation to help the Syrian people by getting some business going so that they wouldn't freeze to death this coming winter and they could grow decent crops this coming spring," Jerry Earnst explained. He was wearing the thickest pair of glasses Linc had ever seen on a human being before.

"How?" Gideon Smith, their second in command, asked.

"High-ranking representatives from Landry Oil and Nutrients Now were meeting with high-level officials from both al-Assad's government and from the Syrian Interim Government. These are opposing forces, but both are very interested in what could be done if they could be helped by these American businesses."

"What happens when they find out that our people are talking to their opposition?" Gideon asked. Lincoln sat forward in his chair.

Yeah, how is Mr. Magoo going to answer that question?

"We have one of our most seasoned diplomats working on this project. Elijah knows how to navigate through treacherous waters. He has set up two different meetings, one in Damascus and one in Aleppo. There is no way for either side to know about the other meeting."

"If this was so foolproof, why do you need us?" Ryker McQueen asked.

Lincoln winced. Trust Ryker to mouth off. But for fuck's sake, not in front of Captain Evers. Linc looked over to where the captain was standing. He had a bird's-eye view of the Omega Sky team and could still see the big flat screen where Jerry was talking. The captain was made of stone. No expression whatsoever. Kind of like their leader, Kostya.

"That explains what we had planned. Now, you taped your two conversations that came in on Leila Cloud's phone. Is that correct, Captain?" Jerry asked.

"Yes."

"There were only two?"

"That's what I said, wasn't it?"

Okay, sometimes Captain Evers could have an expression, and I sure as hell wouldn't want to be the target of his displeasure.

"I just wanted to confirm that I had all of them here," Jerry said. "One was from Leila, and another was from Katherine Cole. She's actually the founder of Nutrients Now."

Jerry leaned into his computer and everybody got a good shot of his nose hair as he fiddled with something on his screen. Then they heard Captain Evers' voice acknowledging Leila Cloud. She immediately explained that they were being held by either ISIS or Al Qaeda, and that their team leader, Elijah Hopkins, had been taken for questioning. They had some weapons, probably from their two dead bodyguards. She said at first that she had six civilians with her, but then she said she had five and one operative. Must have meant that she hadn't realized the fifth man's identity until just that moment. She provided their address, and Evers promised to call back.

Jerry sat back in his chair. "I'm aware of everybody on the team. I know who they are and their backgrounds. Felix Ratcliff was a last-minute replacement for Katherine Cole's head of security. If Leila is talking about an operative, it has to be him. We didn't have time to vet him before the team was put on the plane to Germany."

"You mean to tell me that with all the intelligence you have at your fingertips at Langley, you weren't able to figure out one man's background from the time it took for him to fly from D.C. to Germany? Let alone from Germany to Syria." Kostya's voice could have frozen fire.

Jerry Boy swallowed. "We didn't realize that he was a

replacement until he was on the plane to Syria. At that point, we did a deep dive on him."

"And then?" Gideon asked.

"It wasn't until the team was at the Four Seasons in Damascus that we found out that the real Felix Ratcliff had turned into one of those off-grid people five years ago. It was easy enough for someone to steal his identity. But it doesn't matter, he's dead."

Lincoln sat up straight in his seat.

"The next call came in almost four hours later. This one was from Katherine Cole."

Again, Jerry leaned forward and pressed some keys on his laptop, and then the sound of gunfire filled their ready room.

"Captain Evers?" A woman asked.

"Leila?"

"My name is Katherine Cole. I'm part of Leila's team." There was steel in her voice.

The gunfire ceased.

"We decided to make a break for it, but two of our men have been slaughtered, Landry and Felix. Leila's unconscious and they're dragging her through a pool of blood by her hair. Another man is still alive, but I don't know for how long. They're coming for me and my secretary. Don't call on this phone, I'm hiding it. I'll call you with info as soon as I can."

"Wait!"

"What?"

"Where's Elijah?"

"Don't know. He could still be alive."

The call was disconnected.

Captain Evers stepped forward, blocking the flat screen, which was no hardship. "That was," he looked down at his watch, "fourteen minutes ago."

"Excuse me, Captain, I can't see," Jerry interrupted.

"Elijah has a tracker embedded in his thigh. If we're lucky, he's alive and it won't be found. Leila is former CIA. She doesn't have a tracker embedded, but the phone we kitted her out with is state-of-the art. It can track her."

"All phones come with tracking capabilities," Gideon interrupted. "What's special about this one?"

"It has stingray components."

Gideon whistled. "I didn't know they made stingray components small enough to fit in a smartphone."

"They have." Jerry sounded like he had a woody. "Not only can we track her, but we can track the phones around her. We can listen in. If we get close enough, we can install malware into a phone with sloppy security and turn it into a listening device."

"So, if Katherine can keep the phone hidden long enough, and she's in the presence of the terrorists, not only will we have a location, but we can also find out their intent." Kostya might have only nodded at the information. Gideon's smile was so wide he looked like he was auditioning for a toothpaste commercial.

"That's our plan." Jerry rubbed his hands together as he leaned forward to look at his computer screen.

Gah. Someone really needs to get him a nose hair trimmer.

"So, are they still at the address Leila provided? Who has them? What are their plans?" Gideon asked.

"Umm," Jerry looked at them all. He wasn't talking.

"Mr. Earnest, the man asked you a question," Captain Evers growled. "What intel do you have?"

"Our people here are having a bit of a problem getting readings from Leila's phone. The tracker in Elijah is working just fine. We know they have left the address that

Leila provided and they are on the move. It looks like they are taking the primary avenue that will connect them with either the M5 or 2 highways. That could take them to Aleppo or into ISIS and Al Qaeda territory, or just out of the city. We don't know."

"What are you picking up from Leila's phone, or was it left behind?" Kostya asked.

"No, it's with them. We can tell that it is following the same path as Elijah, but that's it. We're getting so much data coming in, it's impossible to delineate who is saying what, and where the information is coming from. When we got the technology, we were told that we would get phone numbers along with the incoming conversations and locations so that we could tell them apart, but that's not happening."

"When did you start testing this?" Gideon asked.

"That's the thing. We didn't have a chance to test it before we put it into Leila's phone. Our contractor assured us it had passed all of their quality control measures with flying colors. One of my analysts has their chief technology officer on the line. He's thinking it's because of the different types of cell towers that are being used in Syria that we're having problems. That's why there was static on both phone calls to Captain Evers."

Jesus Christ. What were they thinking?

"No field testing was done?" the captain asked.

"Only in the United States."

"Let me get this straight. You sent her out with faulty equipment. Is that what you're telling us?" Kostya asked softly.

"We didn't know it at the time," Jerry defended himself.

"Exactly what did you promise Leila?" Captain Evers asked.

"We told her exactly what I explained to all of you. We said that we basically had a miniaturized stingray unit embedded in her phone."

"So, she's going to be expecting us to not only know exactly where she's at but also who has her, and what they're talking about. Is that correct?"

Jerry said nothing. He just nodded.

"Asshole," Lincoln mumbled to his friend Jase Drakos, who was sitting beside him.

"Tell us what we *do* know," Captain Evers demanded.

"Agent Hopkins—"

"Elijah?" Captain Evers clarified.

"Yes."

"Don't switch names mid-stream," the captain told him.

Jerry nodded.

"We've got a feed here in Langley that shows Elijah's progress. They still haven't made it far enough out of Damascus to determine if they are going to one of the two highways."

"I want that feed sent here," Kostya said.

"We need—" Jerry started.

"All we're asking is that you give us the coded transmission so that we can access the feed. The ship, as well as our team, has the necessary security to keep this information from being breached."

"I can understand sending it to an aircraft carrier, but are you suggesting I send a feed to a deployed Navy SEAL team? That's preposterous."

"Seems to me like your feed isn't worth a shit, so why should you care?" Jase Drakos drawled.

Linc kept his features neutral, and he noticed everybody in the room did, too, including the captain. It was good old Jerry who looked ready to blow a gasket.

"We're going to get this worked out. We've already demanded that they get their development team here immediately to work on this situation. The chief technology officer has promised to come to Langley. They'll be here tomorrow morning."

"Meanwhile, your team could be dead by then," Kostya said. "Send the feed." He stood up and looked at Captain Evers.

"You heard the man establish two channels." Evers glared at the screen. "I want it done in less than an hour. These men will be heading in."

"I'm not sure we can get that done in an hour," good ole Jerry admitted.

"Yes, you can. If you can't, fire yourself and have your boss hire someone who can." The captain picked up the remote and turned off the screen. He turned to the second in command on their team, Gideon Smith. "I've heard good things about you, Smith. Come with me, and I'll have you meet some of the people who work in comms. I think you might enjoy checking out some of our equipment."

Even from the back row, it was easy to see Gideon's grin. He might be a SEAL, but he was a tech geek at heart.

"Kostya, you have the mission plans on getting into either Lebanon, Syria, or Turkey. Why don't you run through those and tell me what you need."

"Will do." Kostya nodded as the captain and Gideon left the room. Their lieutenant turned his attention back to them. "Since Gideon decided to go play, you're stuck with me running things." Kostya opened up the laptop that Gideon had left at his seat and started keying. He only swore once before he picked up the remote control that the captain had used to turn off the monitor. The screen fired up and there was a map of Syria, along with a cursor.

"We have three different plans to infiltrate Syria, depending on where we want to go."

Lincoln looked at the map. He'd been betting that they were going to Turkey; showed how little he knew. The fact that either of the two countries was busy with internal political power plays when they were still dealing with catastrophic human and infrastructure losses after the earthquake was unbelievable.

"Where are you thinking they're headed?" Ryker asked their lieutenant.

Kostya gave him the side-eye.

"Yeah," Ryker grinned. "It'll be Highway 2 or Highway 7. Either will get them started to Northeast Syria."

Everyone around in the room nodded.

"But in case we're wrong and they don't head to northeastern Syria, where ISIS and Al Qaeda have a stronghold, we need to be able to pivot to the M5 heading toward Aleppo."

"And if they stay in Damascus?" Matteo Arranda asked.

"Even better. Shorter amount of time we have to be searching for them." Kostya said.

Ryker McQueen raised his hand.

Kostya gave him a chin tilt.

"Excuse me, lieutenant. When did you get taken over by aliens? I'm pretty sure I heard you say something positive. You can't be the Kostya Barona I've worked for these past four years."

Kostya rubbed the back of his neck and the left side of his mouth kicked up so that he was almost smiling. "Things change."

"So, you were taken over by aliens. Did you get probed?" Jase Drakos asked. "I've always wanted to know. Were they little green men, or tall skinny gray men?"

Kostya rolled his eyes heavenward. "Fine. In an effort to get this meeting back on track, I'll tell you. Lark's pregnant. She just hit week thirteen. She said we could tell people now. She's had me on pins and needles with this 'first twelve weeks things could go wrong' bullshit. Now life is good, gentleman. It's really, really good."

"That's damn good news. Congratulations, Kostya," Linc got up from his seat and held out his hand. He felt the rest of the team lining up behind him. Linc put his hand on Kostya's shoulder. "Seriously, Kostya. I can't think of many men who could make a better father. Your kid has hit the jackpot already."

Kostya's eyes flared for just a moment, then his grin got bigger. "Thanks, Linc, means a lot."

"Hey, get out of the way," Ryker said as he jostled past him. "Lots of others who want to congratulate the baby daddy."

Linc stepped back to watch the others give their good wishes. Kostya moved things along at a quick clip and got everybody's ass back in their seats in less than three minutes. "Captain Evers has a Black Hawk waiting for us. We just have to determine where we want it to take us. I've been in touch with Lieutenant Rankin, who runs a platoon of Marines out of Al Tanf Garrison. He's going to support us."

Kostya zoomed in to where the garrison was located. "The garrison is almost at the end of Hwy 2 in Syria, but it wouldn't make sense for the kidnappers to take them to the west of Syria, unless they want to take them into Iraq. Jerry, our current CIA liaison," Kostya put an emphasis on the word current, "doesn't think the hostages will be taken to Iraq. I agree with him. We're on better terms with Iraq than we are Syria. Al-Assad only allows our troops in his country so that we can help him minimize the ISIS and Al Qaeda threats from the northeast."

"Is Rankin providing us with transport?" Jase asked. He was Omega Sky's tracker. If you were in the middle of nowhere or in the middle of downtown Manhattan, Jase could find you. Of course, Gideon's magical intel never hurt.

"Yes. He told me to call in after I had the map up and had a chance to look at it. Hold on."

He pulled out his cell phone and placed the call.

"Rankin here. This Barona?"

"Yep, you've got me and my team."

"Sergeant Wilcox is with me. Do you know where your targets are right now?"

"If they're still together, they're on the M5, but it's slow going. So's Highway 2. At the rate they're going, it'll take forty-five minutes before they get to Baghdad Bridge. At that point, they could switch over to Highway 2."

"Wilcox, tell him your plan," Rankin said.

"We can have vehicles waiting for you on the M5, Highway 7, as well as at Highway 2. They'll be far enough away from Damascus that you'll be able to wait and pick them up. Your choice whether you want to do the rescue or follow."

"My men can't be part of the mission," Rankin put in.

"Understood," Kostya said. He looked up as Gideon stepped back into the conference room. "We'll be taking off in twenty minutes. While we're en route, we should know whether they're taking the M5 to Aleppo or they're taking Highway 7 or Highway 2 to ISIS and Al Qaeda territory."

Linc watched as Gideon took a quick look at the map and nodded at Kostya. He understood what Kostya was saying.

"I'm also going to talk to the Syrian commander here and explain we're using Black Hawk here to do some training, and that one will be sent in from the aircraft carrier," Rankin said.

"And when we don't take a direct route to the garrison?" Kostya asked.

"I'll come up with something."

Linc was pretty sure he heard Rankin's sergeant laugh in the background.

"I'll get back to you when we have more information," Kostya assured the lieutenant.

"In the meantime, my men will head out. How many men will you be bringing?"

"Eight."

"We'll bring two vehicles for you to each site."

"Obliged."

"Safe travels," Rankin said before hanging up.

Kostya turned to his team. "Get suited up and meet me up on the flight deck in fifteen minutes. I want these people found and returned before tomorrow. Got it?"

Everybody nodded and got up from their chairs, as they responded 'yes' or 'got it'.

Linc wasn't surprised to see Gideon hang back with their lieutenant.

4

THE HAND-OFF TO THE HUMVEES HAD BEEN EASY. THE TEAM had pulled off at an electrical power station before the small town of Al Qaryatayn. This way, they could easily do a roadblock.

"Big doings in Quarry Town," Jase said.

"I don't know. I saw the truck of chickens go by twenty minutes ago. It looked like they might be having a party." Ryker smirked.

"What do you think of the boss being a dad?" Linc asked the car in general.

"Have you seen him with his niece and nephew?" Mateo asked. "I did. I was at the carnival with someone, and I saw him with two kids who looked just like him. It was clear they adored him."

"Someone?" Linc asked, his eyebrows raised almost to his hairline. "When was this?"

"Two, maybe three years ago."

"What was her name?" Linc persisted.

"I can't remember her name. Like I said, it was two or three years ago," Mateo protested.

"Cut the guy some slack," Ryker chided Linc. "Three years in Mateo time means thirty-six months. Three months per woman, means twelve women. How can his brain be expected to remember that many names?"

Everybody laughed, especially Jase.

"Don't be laughing too hard, Drakos," Matteo called out to his friend. "You're just as bad."

"I used to be. Haven't you noticed? I've sobered up. I've taken a sabbatical."

"Oh really? Since last week?" Matteo chortled.

"Actually, it's been almost a year. The last couple of women I dated were just women I dated. They weren't people I would ever want to call a friend. I really didn't enjoy their company all that much. What was the point?"

"Uhhhhm, to get laid?" Matteo pointed out.

"I can date my right hand and spend less money, have less hassle, and a lot of times have a better time."

"Damn, that's harsh."

"That's what I thought. It's the reason I'm on a sabbatical. I think part of it was seeing Nolan, Kostya, and Gideon pairing off. They found some good women, so I know they're out there. Now I want a shot."

Everything Jase was saying resonated with Linc.

Every.

Damn.

Word.

Well, if he'd been doing the talking, he might not have mentioned the hand part.

"Fuck it's hot," Matteo murmured.

"I think I remember you bitching about the cold in Finland. So, which is it? Do you like the cold or the heat?" Ryker asked.

"Oh, he just likes to bitch," Jase laughed. "He's the

common denominator on why the women don't last. He doesn't scrape them off, they dump him."

Linc laughed along with everyone else as Matteo frowned.

"Come on, man, he has a point. You do see things from a glass is half empty point of view," Linc pointed out.

"I—"

"Five kilometers out. Start your engines." Gideon's voice came through their comm system.

"Roger that," Linc answered. He was the driver, so he started the engine.

Jonas was driving the other vehicle. He was behind him. He always preferred to be in front, but you couldn't have everything. He should just be happy that his leg was doing so damned well after the bullet he'd taken in Russia. A half smile tipped his lips. He'd made a damn good shot, though. Saved their asses. That's what really mattered.

"Leila's shitty phone should be pinging by now. We still only have Elijah's tracker," Gideon said grimly.

Linc could feel the mood in the car amp up. Everybody was on alert.

"Maybe they found it and got rid of it," Landon Kelly said from the other car. He was the youngest teammate. Where Matteo was a glass half empty kind of guy, Landon's glass was half full and the glass was made with rose-tinted glass. Linc knew the day would come when Landon's glass would shatter. He hated to think about it.

"It could be anything," Kostya said. "We've only seen three vehicles in the time we've been here, which is almost an hour. Linc, cross the highway and on my mark, you'll come out and block that side, we'll block this side.

Use the rear of your vehicles so we can be prepared to follow them if they go off-road."

"Got it." He veered past Jonas's Humvee and crossed over the highway. He found two scraggly bushes that might hide a child, but they were the best camouflage he had available, so he parked his vehicle behind it, the rear end facing the road. He looked in his rearview mirror and saw that Jonas had done the same thing, only he was still behind the electrical power station.

"Two klicks out," Gideon reported. Linc looked out of his window. He couldn't see their vehicle yet. He started counting in his head. When he reached eleven, he saw a vehicle. He saw two vehicles. *Shit!* Was one a civilian?

He thought about who the living players were. Elijah Hopkins, Leila Cloud, Katherine Cole and her secretary Annie Trent, and Sam Phelps the former Marine. Okay, that many would account for two vehicles.

He pulled up his binoculars. The first was a car, looked to be a little Russian OKA, and behind them was a tarp-covered truck. The OKA could comfortably seat one as far as Linc was concerned, but he'd seen places across the Middle East where they'd crowded families of eight or nine into the vehicle. When he zoomed in with his binoculars, he could tell that the front seat only had the driver, a passenger, and two rifles. He couldn't tell who or what was in the backseat.

They were moving slowly, probably in deference to the big truck behind them. When he tipped his binoculars upward, he saw that there was only one man in the cab of the truck. He didn't see any rifle standing up beside him. Maybe he had all of his guns stashed on his empty passenger seat.

"Gideon, are you getting a good view? I only see the

passenger and driver in the car, and just a driver in the truck. What about you?"

"Same."

"How are we playing it?"

Linc's question was met by silence. He knew why. Rankin had loaded them up when it came to what they were driving. They hadn't skimped in the slightest. Linc and Jonas were both driving advanced up-armored Humvees with armored gun turrets, just in case the kids started fighting in the backseat and you needed to send them upstairs to play.

"Landon and Ryker, I want you both up top," Kostya said through the comm. "I want Mateo and me at the back bumpers in the center of the highway."

"Are you thinking they're a package deal?" Linc asked his lieutenant.

"Pretty sure," Kostya replied. "Even if they're not, no harm, no foul. We stop them both. Let me know when you're in position." Ryker was in the turret in less than sixty seconds.

"Beat you," he crowed over the comm. "Experience once again beats youth."

"Asshole," Landon muttered.

"On my mark," Kostya said.

Linc looked over at Jase, who was in the passenger seat. He didn't have a good view of the road. He looked back over his shoulder at Mateo. "You got 'em?" he asked.

"Yep," Mateo answered.

"Good." Linc shoved his binoculars into his chest pack and started up the engine, and shoved it into reverse. He was ready.

"Now!" Kostya growled into the comm.

He couldn't see the target, all he was concentrating on

was backing up onto the highway so that he could blockade it without jamming into the vehicle that Jonas was driving. Linc grinned when they both stopped, mere inches between their vehicles.

He whipped his head around and grinned again. The OKA couldn't stop in time. It veered to the right, its bumper hitting his Humvee, then pinged off it like a pinball and twirled so that the side of the car slammed into Jonas' vehicle. The truck behind tried to stop in time, even from where he was, behind his closed window. Linc could smell the burning rubber as the truck did its best to stop. At the last minute, it took a hard right to avoid the metal barrier in front of it, aiming for the sand on the side of the highway. Linc watched as the truck started to tip. Even from where he was sitting, he could see the panic on the driver's face. He winced when the truck crashed onto its side.

"Linc, you and your men take the truck. We'll check out the car and then be with you," Kostya ordered.

Linc was out of their vehicle before he knew what he was doing. Years of training kicking in. His rifle was up and ready. He heard gunshots behind him, but he didn't react. His attention was on the truck and the driver who was fumbling for his rifle.

"Stop. Hands up." That was Jase behind him. His Arabic was the best in his vehicle. The driver continued to go for his rifle. He started to raise it. Linc shot him in the head. The four of them didn't even need to discuss who went right and who went left; again all their time training and working together took over. They worked like a well-oiled machine. Linc had Matteo with him on the left and Jase was taking the right side.

"Landon. Ryker. Anything from your POV?" Kostya asked the men in the turrets.

"Negative," they both answered.

"Ours are down. We're coming in from the right. The three of you take the left," Kostya ordered. "You know what to do."

There wasn't a chance in hell they were just going to head to the end of the truck like lambs to slaughter. Linc slid his knife out of its sheath and silently cut into the tarp where it met the cab. He lifted it just enough so he could see in. It was dark, and it took a moment for his eyes to adjust.

Three men were crouched down. One had his automatic rifle pointed at what was once the ceiling.

"Rifle pointed your way," he whispered almost silently into his mic. "Middle of truck."

"Understood." Kostya's whisper was barely heard, but Linc knew he was moving his team.

One of the three men had his rifle pointed toward the mouth of the truck entrance, ready for an attack. The third man had his rifle pointed at a young woman. She had pale blonde hair. Not Leila. She and two men were tied up. Why they bothered with the men was beyond him. They were unconscious and looked like they had been beaten within an inch of their lives. The woman's blouse was in tatters and her bra only covered one breast, but at least her slacks were still on.

The terrorists started whispering. Loud enough that Linc could hear, but not understand.

Linc tilted his head at Jase. He came over and took Linc's place.

Jase listened for a couple of minutes, then backed up so that he could report to everyone. "They think al-Assad's men have surrounded them. They want to trade the people in the truck for safe passage back to Al Hasakah."

"Who do they have in the truck?" Kostya asked.

"The two men, and the blonde. I think that's Katherine Cole's secretary," Jase answered.

"That would explain why we haven't gotten any signals from Leila's piece of shit phone." Gideon's voice was filled with disgust.

Gunshots filled the air.

"Go time," Kostya bit out.

Jase fired into the truck as Linc ripped back the tarp to let in more light. He saw light coming in from the other side. Two men down.

Shit!

Instead of a rifle at Annie's gut, the third guy now had a knife at her throat. Blood dripped down her tattered blouse and chest.

Fuck!

Jase yelled something to him in Arabic, and he screamed back.

Linc and Jase had rifles pointed at him. Then there were Kostya and Ryker behind him, waiting to shoot. It was a no-win situation. That knife was at her jugular.

She was still, her expression flat, but those blue eyes told Linc she was ready to die.

Jase started talking again. Instead of yelling, he sounded like one of the horsemen of the apocalypse. Linc could see the whites of the man's eyes. The knife lifted, just a little.

As the team's sniper, he didn't carry the normal automatic rifle that everybody else had. He packed an MK13 sniper rifle. A rifle that he'd spent months training with and years working with, but at such close quarters it was useless. Showing almost no movement at all, he pulled out his Sig Sauer, and flicked off the safety. He brought the gun up so that he had a level shot.

"Again," Linc ordered Jase. "I need another quarter of an inch."

Jase glanced over at him and saw what he was doing. Jase moved to his right so the terrorist would keep his eyes on him and not pay attention to Linc and his pistol. Jase snarled out something that had even Linc shivering. Apparently, his teammate was wasted in special forces. He should've been in Hollywood.

Linc's concentration was focused on the hand holding the knife. The fingers, gripping the blade. His grimy thumb and forefinger were now trembling. Linc waited for his chance. The knife lifted just a little, and he took the shot. Fingers and handle blew apart... blew backward as a fine mist of blood hit the air.

A loud rip screeched along with the terrorist's shriek as Jonas, Kostya, and Gideon piled through what was once the tarp roof of the truck.

Jonas got to the terrorist first, grabbing him by the throat and throwing him against the steel floor as he checked him for weapons.

"Mateo," Kostya shouted, but it wasn't necessary. He had already hauled himself up and over the side of the truck and was checking out the two unconscious men. He looked over his shoulder at Annie, but saw that Kostya was talking to her.

"Nice shot," Gideon said as he sidled up to Linc.

Linc nodded. "Where are the other two? Katherine and Leila?" Linc asked the young woman. They all turned to look at the crying terrorist, who was currently trying to stop Jonas from stepping on what was left of his hand.

"I think it was the leader who took them," Annie whispered. Linc, Kostya and Ryker heard her since they were close.

Linc saw Ryker buttoning up his camouflage shirt over his bare chest as Kostya was gently helping Annie into what had to be Ryker's sweaty T-shirt. Even from where Linc was standing, he could tell that, sweaty or not, she was grateful to be covered.

"Why do you think that?" Linc asked as he crouched down in front of the young woman.

"Because he was the one who first talked to us and took Elijah away. He's the only one who spoke English. Why would they have taken Mrs. Cole?"

Linc looked up at the sound of puking. He expected it to be the terrorist, but it wasn't. It was one of the two men that Mateo was working on. He had him rolled over so he wouldn't drown on his own vomit.

With his face a pulpy mess, it was hard to discern who he was. Linc looked over at the other man and realized he was bigger and in better shape. He'd bet the farm that he was the former Marine. Therefore, this guy must be Elijah Hopkins.

"Fuck me," he heard the man rasp.

"What's your name?" Mateo asked as he prodded the man's naked chest. He looked grim.

It took forever for the man to answer. "Hopkins. You're American. Am I still in Syria?"

"Yes, Sir," Mateo answered.

Since Annie had stopped talking, Linc and everyone but Jonas turned their attention to Elijah.

"You're still in Syria," Kostya answered. "I'm Kostya Barona, Lieutenant in the US Navy."

"SEAL?" Elijah asked.

"Yes," Kostya answered.

"You found me through my tracker. Good. What's the situation?"

"Sam Phelps needs a hospital. Now," Mateo said. "So do you. You have a punctured lung, and if I had to guess, you have internal bleeding. We can operate on the aircraft carrier. I don't know what can be done at the outpost."

Elijah slumped and closed his eyes. Linc thought he'd passed out, but then he started to talk again. "Besides Phelps, who made it out?"

"Annie Trent, Leila Cloud, and Katherine Cole. We only have Annie, Sam, and you. We're trying to discern where Katherine and Leila are," Kostya answered.

At that news, Elijah opened his eyes. "And the others? Landry? Felix?"

Kostya shook his head. "Dead."

Hopkins nodded.

"Lieutenant," Mateo interrupted. "Sam needs surgery, or he's going to die. Every minute counts."

Kostya nodded. Both men looked over at Gideon, who was on his satellite phone. He was looking grim. When he hung up, he looked at Mateo and Kostya, shaking his head.

"No helicopters. Al-Assad's men bought into the Black Hawk flying over their lands once instead of heading northeast, but they made it clear if our people did it again, they'd shoot it down."

"Okay, I'll do my best to get them ready for transport on the Humvees," Mateo nodded before Kostya could even ask the question.

Linc looked over at his boss. His face wasn't giving anything away, but his frustration was coming off him in waves. Nolan O'Roarke was their normal medic, and he'd given him to Night Storm for a mission because their medic had a broken arm and their back-up medic was too integral to their mission to do any kind of medical work.

Then there was the fact that *their* back-up medic was back in Virginia getting his ass kicked with the other members of Omega Sky in jungle warfare training. That left Mateo, with no back-up to care for two critically injured men to get to safety.

"Here's the play," Kostya hollered. "We don't have enough room for everybody to ride to the Al Tanf Outpost. Mateo, you're going to go with Phelps in the backseat of one Humvee. Is it going to kill him to sit up?"

"I don't know," Mateo admitted. "If the seatbelt tightens around his lower abdomen, I think that could."

"Understood."

"Ryker, you're with Elijah. Cut the bottom of both their seatbelts. I'm driving you, Annie will be in the passenger seat. Jonas will drive the other vehicle with Landon in the passenger seat, then Mateo and Phelps in the back."

The Omega Sky team nodded.

He gave Linc, Jase, and Gideon a hard glance. "Al Qaryatayn is less than six klicks. You should be able to pick up some kind of transport after it gets dark. Jase, I'm leaving Jonas' new friend with you since you can speak Arabic. If you get intel from him, report it to me. Likewise, if I hear anything from Elijah, I'll get it back to you."

It was a solid plan. Linc liked it.

He watched as Ryker took Elijah with Kostya's help, then Mateo took Sam with Landon's help. Linc and Gideon ran forward and opened the doors of the vehicles, helping to get the injured men safely ensconced in their seats.

As they drove off, the rumble of Jase's voice could be

heard. Linc started forward, while Gideon went to the OKA.

"What are you doing?" Linc asked.

"I'm going to see if there is any fucking way I can track that phone. I'll check in with Langley and see if that idiot CTO is there yet and what he's come up with. Then I'll check in with some of the other SEAL team computer techs and get them on the job, too."

"And bloody seats seem like a good place to work?"

Gideon looked over his shoulder and shook his head. "There's a back seat. But I am getting rid of the corpses. Can't say I really want to be working with two stiffs."

"I'll help."

Linc jogged over to the driver's side of the small car and yanked the door open. He pulled out the driver. He'd been shot in the head. Looking in the back seat, he could see a mess that Gideon might not want to be working in.

After pulling the driver out of the car, he pulled off his shirt and found a fairly clean part and used it to wipe off the back seat. Linc looked up and saw that Gideon was doing the same thing with the passenger.

"Okay, I'm all set."

"Good luck. I just sure as shit hope that they still have the phone with them."

5

THIS IS NOT GOOD.

Not good at all.

A man that Leila didn't recognize came into the room. He was wearing a suit and tie. Not just any suit. This suit had obviously been tailored to fit him. Now *this* man looked like *he* was in charge. He walked calmly into one of the innocuous empty offices where she was currently tied to a chair. He was holding a piece of paper.

"Tell me why you're here, Leila Cloud, translator," he said as he looked down at the piece of paper in his hand.

"I'm a freelance translator. I was hired by Elijah Hopkins to help explore opportunities between the al-Assad regime and two American companies."

"America has a policy of not doing business with Syria. Do you expect me to believe you?"

"It's the truth."

He looked back down at the piece of paper in his hand and nodded.

"Had you done work with Elijah Hopkins before?" he asked curiously.

"Yes. He and my father went to school together. I probably work for him once a year."

"And why was your team meeting in this government building today, and not back at your hotel?"

"We were told that members of the al-Assad government would meet us here."

"And when your meeting room blew up? What did you think, then?"

"I thought that members of ISIS or Al Qaeda were trying to stop the meeting. That was another part of the reason we were doing this in secret," Leila answered honestly.

The man nodded. Then slapped the piece of paper onto the desk. "I have some questions for you, Leila Cloud. Freelance Translator. Currently completing your master's degree in Global Affairs in Turkey as you live with your grandparents."

Holy hell, how does he know that?

The man continued. "After only two years of college at Georgetown University, you went to work as an analyst with America's Central Intelligence Agency before going back to complete your degree in communications."

He looked up from the sheet of paper and his grin was positively feral. Where had he gotten that information? She had never posted her time with the CIA on the web.

"Ah, you're getting curious. I see it in your eyes. Let me continue. It says here that you aren't just fluent in Arabic, but that you can read and write in Arabic. Is that true?"

Leila said nothing.

"Answer me," he demanded in Arabic, his fist hitting the table so hard that it jumped.

"Yes," she answered in English.

"Arabic. You will speak to me in Arabic."

"Yes," Leila said in Arabic. "I'm fluent in Arabic."

"And what other languages?" he continued in Arabic.

Leila swallowed. He was looking at the damned piece of paper. She rarely put down every language that she spoke. She would write down the languages relevant to the position that she was applying for, otherwise it seemed to intimidate potential employers.

"I speak Arabic, English, Turkish and French," she answered.

He slapped her so hard across the face that both she and the chair she was tied to fell over and slid at least four feet across the tiled floor.

"Don't lie to me again. I know everything."

If you know everything, you wouldn't be questioning me, you asshole.

Leila had just the smallest amount of restraint to not say those words out loud, although she could feel her cheek swelling up and her ears were ringing.

He pushed at the office chair with the tip of his wingtip shoe. It slid further across the floor. "I'll ask again. What other languages do you speak?"

"Russian." Her voice was garbled by the hit. "Portuguese."

"There, was that really so hard?"

He grabbed the rope that lashed her upper body to the chair and yanked. Leila's head flopped from the sudden move, and pain seared down from her head to her neck, then down her spine. She couldn't help but groan.

He picked up the paper from the desk.

"What did you do when you were with the CIA?"

This time, she told the truth. "I sat in a cubicle and translated documents. It was a boring job."

"Did you ever go out into the field?"

"Can I have some water?"

"After you answer my questions."

Leila started to cough. What started out as just a little playacting soon turned into a real coughing fit. He stared at her dispassionately.

The coughing aggravated her injuries and her eyes began to water.

I will not cry in front of this bastard. I won't.

Finally, she stopped coughing and she choked back the tears.

"What is it you want with me? Where are the others?"

This time, he rephrased the question and it sent a shiver down her spine. "Tell me about your mission with the CIA."

There was no way he should have known about that. No way. She'd never even told her dad, and he was FBI. Obviously, they had a traitor in the CIA, and that's why this entire operation had gone to shit.

"Leila, I asked you a question."

Her cheek throbbed. "I only went on a mission one time. After that, I quit."

"What happened?"

"I was just supposed to be the translator for a meeting in Kazakhstan. It was supposed to be a pre-meeting before we sent out our diplomats; instead it was an ambush. As we were getting off the train, three of our men were shot, and if it hadn't been for Agent Perkins getting the two of us back onto the train and hidden in a sleeper coach, we would have been killed too."

"Do you know why this happened?"

"Nobody ever told me."

The man nodded.

"So, eight years later, you decided to blindly trust

someone from the CIA when he asks you to act as a translator for a job in Syria. Do you expect me to believe that?"

"He's a friend of my father's. They went to school together. He's also my godfather."

"That wasn't my question." He put the paper down on the table again and took a step closer to her. Now he was standing over her and she had to lean her head backward to look into his face.

"A woman who was almost killed on her first mission with the CIA would not go out on another mission without all the facts. Tell me what you know about being here in Syria."

Leila thought fast. Somebody on the inside had been feeding him information. It couldn't have been Elijah, otherwise they would have never hauled him out of the room like they had. So did this guy know about the operation? Know about the diamonds?

"Leila, answer me!" Again, he pounded on the desk.

"I know Elijah was supposed to be discussing how to free some prisoners that are currently being held by al-Assad. I swear, that's all I know."

She bit her lip, praying he would believe her.

He grabbed her by her hair and twisted.

"I don't believe you. I know he was doing something more than negotiating. I think there was some kind of payment involved. I want to know what it was, and where it is."

She cried out when he pulled her—and the chair up —by her hair. Tears formed.

"Tell me," he whispered. "Just take a moment to catch your breath, and tell me."

Nothing made sense. If this guy was getting info from

a spy at Langley, wouldn't he know about the CIA operative here in Syria who was holding onto the diamonds?

"I don't know."

"Tell me!"

Leila swore she could feel her scalp beginning to bleed.

"I don't know."

"Tell me."

"If I tell you, you'll kill me," she gasped.

He let go, and she crashed to the floor.

Air gusted in and out of her chest. Her head dropped forward and this time she couldn't stop the tears.

"Was that really so hard? Who were the prisoners? Who was Elijah going to pay? What was the payment? Where is it?"

"Three reporters and an aid worker," Leila whispered.

The man rattled off the four names, and Leila nodded.

"Who in al-Assad's government was going to do the trade?"

She knew that if she told him, she was signing the man's death warrant. Or maybe this terrorist would turn him into his own spy.

She kept her mouth shut. He slapped her again, this time on the other cheek. Again, she and the chair went down. She screamed as her previously wounded cheek scraped against the tiled floor.

"You will tell me."

His voice came from a long way away. Leila felt fuzzy.

"What is his name?"

She felt his hand grab the rope and pull her up. This time, when her head flopped forward and the searing pain hit her head and neck, she lost focus and...nothing.

"HE KNOWS NOTHING," Jase said, disgustedly.

"Useless," Linc agreed as he stared down at the crying man. "Damn, you're scary, Jase. I don't know what the hell you said, but he actually pissed his pants."

"Easy. I told him Jonas was coming back to step on his hand. Didn't matter though, all we heard is how he'd failed in his mission and he was going to be killed, so we might as well kill him."

Linc pursed his lips and shook his head. Wasn't the first time they'd heard that from an al Qaeda prisoner.

"So our only hope is that Elijah will have an idea where they've taken Leila and Katherine Cole or that the two women have held onto the phone and Gideon can track it."

Jase nodded. "Seems like."

"And him?" Linc asked as he tilted his chin toward the man sobbing against the side of the truck.

"I don't know. What do you think?"

"The two cars that have come down this road have just driven on past this truck."

Jase nodded. "It was a good call on your part to push the OKA back behind the electrical power station. If people saw the truck and the OKA, they might have stopped."

"Doubt it." Linc hit his mic. "You got anything for us, Gideon?"

"Maybe. I'm not sure. I need at least another hour."

"Understood."

"I checked in with Kostya," Gideon continued. "Elijah has been unconscious the entire trip, to Al Tanf he never regained consciousness, so we got nothing."

"Are you saying he's dead?" Linc asked.

"Shit, I said it wrong. No he's still alive, just not awake to tell us anything," Gideon clarified.

"Dammit."

Linc looked over at his friend. It was now ten o'clock in the evening. If they stayed away from the road, nobody should spot them as they made their way to Al Qaryatayn.

"Let's tie him up and head to town and grab a vehicle," Linc said as he stared at the prisoner.

"Sounds good."

After they got him gagged and zip-tied, they went over to Gideon. "What are you working on?" Linc asked.

"I've fed what I've got over to Clint Archer from Midnight Delta. He has deep connections with a big player in the wireless telecommunications field in San Diego. He's already shared the schematics of the piece of shit stingray that Jerry Earnst gave Leila and they're reverse engineering it to see how they can make it work."

"That's great and all," Jase said. "But we don't have the phone."

"Really?" Gideon asked. "You're right, we didn't think of that."

Jase sighed. Jase had walked right into that one.

Gideon went on to explain. "If they can reverse engineer it, the guys Clint's involved with think they may have a way to get it to work if they can just get a connection to the phone. She's going to have to call them, or she's going to have to pick up their call to make this work."

"What about what Jerry-Boy told us regarding the Syrian cellphone networks here in Syria not being compatible with this software? How are they going to fix *that* problem?" Linc asked.

"When I had a chance to look at the schematics, it was pretty clear that the stingray itself was fucked up. I reviewed them with Clint and he agreed, and that's when he pulled in his buddies. Now, the Syrian network should not be a problem, because she has a satellite phone. The network was only an issue when they tried to dick with the stingray components."

"And Clint and his buddies can get that fixed?" Linc asked.

Gideon shook his head.

"Then what the fuck can they do?" Linc wanted to know.

"We track her. Apparently, this company in San Diego has been working to make their products stingray-resistant. Therefore, they know stingray technology inside, outside, and sideways. But goddammit, they won't be able to make her phone work the way it's supposed to. I'm so mad at those motherfuckers who sent her out with faulty equipment. She would have been so much better off with just a normal satellite phone and a tracker, but no, they had to give her a phone with all the bells and whistles that jacked up just normal tracking capabilities. The motherfuckers."

Linc waited for Gideon to calm down and asked his question again.

"How are you going to get rid of all the shit on her phone and get the tracking working?"

"As soon as she calls in to Evers, they have a patch that they'll run. It'll wipe out all the stingray software and allow the tracker to work."

"Why the fuck did they even want the stringray components in the phone to begin with?" Jase asked. "What does it do?"

"It allows her to record phone calls in her proximity and download texts. She can also install malware on a phone and take the phone over, allowing her to make outgoing calls on the phone or do outgoing texts."

"Are you shitting me?" Jase asked.

"Nope. That tech has been around for a while. It's just big and cumbersome. Nobody has figured out how to install it into something small and portable like a phone, before."

Enough already!

"Gideon, love hearing about all the bells and whistles, but...

Are.

You.

Sure.

We.

Can.

Track.

Her?"

Gideon scrubbed his hand over his shaved head.

"If we can just get her to call us or take a call, it's a done deal." It was clear that Gideon was as frustrated as Linc was.

"Who is us? She's called Captain Evers. Have you arranged it if she calls into him, that you can install the patch?"

"That's the next step. Linc, you've got to trust me. We're working every angle."

Linc blew out a deep breath.

"You had a thing for her during that Turkey mission, didn't you?" Gideon asked.

"Yes, he did," Jase answered for him. "But it really

doesn't matter. He'd be this pissed about anybody we were trying to rescue."

"Gideon's right," Linc said, turning to Jase. "Normally I *wouldn't* be this emotional about the whole thing." He turned and faced his second-in-command. "Yeah, after that whole mission, I tried to look her up when we got back home, but I couldn't find her. I thought about having you track her down for me, but I figured there was a reason she needed to go to ground, so I left it."

"Fuck. Is this going to make things more complicated?" Gideon asked.

"It won't," Linc assured him.

It won't, he assured himself.

But an image of her long, lean body and warm bronze skin with her dark eyes flashed in his mind. How often *had* he thought about her? *Too fucking often.*

"I need another hour to work this out."

"Then we're out of here. We'll go on to Al Qaryatayn and pick up a vehicle, and come back."

"Our friend in the truck?" Gideon asked.

"He should be good for another day or two. It's March. He won't freeze or die of heat stroke before someone gets to him."

Gideon nodded, then turned back to his computer.

"Let's move on down the road," Jase said.

6

I FEEL WORSE THAN WHEN I WAS IN THE WRECK ON THE Capital Beltway.

Leila tried to push herself up from the metal floor, but she just didn't have the strength in her arms.

"Easy."

Leila shook her head, trying to pinpoint who the voice belonged to, but before she could, the floor shook and her arms went out from underneath her and she landed hard on her chest and face. She didn't even have the strength to cry out.

"Leila, don't move until I come over and help you."

Katherine. It was Katherine Cole.

"Where are we?"

"In a truck. We were both thrown in here," the woman paused. "Three hours and twenty minutes ago."

A soft hand pushed back her hair and probed her cheek.

She moaned.

"Dammit, I should have done this when you were

passed out. Hold still, I want to see if your cheekbone is broken."

"I don't think so. I can talk."

Katherine actually chuckled. "My son used to ride dirt bikes. Trust me, it doesn't matter if you can talk, your cheekbone can still be broken."

Leila took in a deep breath and held it. She thought of the cherry blossoms in Washington, D.C., and imagined herself under one of the trees as the petals drifted down on her.

"Let me get you into a seated position, then I can check the other side of your face."

"Katherine, it doesn't matter. What matters is getting the hell out of here. Do you still have the phone?"

"I turned it off. There was hardly any charge left."

Leila nodded, then hissed at the pain in her neck that radiated throughout her body. "Okay, you're already hurting. Let's get this done."

Katherine pulled her up and, with her help, she could scrabble backward and sit up against the hard metal of the moving vehicle. She could barely make out Katherine's visage.

"How many men are we dealing with?" she asked.

"At first I thought it was one of the terrorist groups, but there's this man in a suit," Katherine answered. "He doesn't make sense. He's being driven in a Mercedes behind the truck. The others all look like militants."

"How many?" Leila asked again, trying to consider their options.

"I'm not sure in this truck, at least the driver. But there were three others besides the suit in the Mercedes."

"Can you please give me the phone?" Leila asked.

Katherine chuckled. "I love the please during this shitshow. Somebody raised you right," she said as she pressed the phone into Leila's hands.

Leila hurt too much to laugh, but yeah, her *nene* would slap her hand with a spoon if she didn't say please and thank you.

She keyed in the phone number she had memorized.

Before the phone had even completed ringing, Captain Evers was saying her name.

"Leila, do you know where you are?"

Her stomach plummeted.

Every ache and pain stopped. It felt like her very life had stopped as she replayed his question in her mind.

"How come you don't know where I am?" Her voice was flat.

Katherine grabbed her thigh; her nails dug so deep Leila thought she might leave tiny bruises.

"There's a problem with your phone. It's not working right in Syria. Something to do with the cellphone towers."

"Will it be fixed?"

"We're working on it. The ETA is sixty minutes."

"Captain, I'm with Katherine Cole. I don't know where the others are. We've kept this phone on because it was supposed to have all the capabilities explained to me. The battery is very low. I don't have sixty minutes to leave it on. Hell, I don't know if I have sixty minutes before the terrorists take us out of the truck and do whatever they have planned."

She heard him whisper, "Fuck."

"Can you memorize a phone number if I give it to you?"

"Yes. That I can do."

He gave her the number.

"How much juice do you have? Can you check in every fifteen minutes?"

"I'm at six percent. The problem is with all this software loaded on the phone, I don't have any idea how fast I'm losing power." She tried to make out the face of her watch, but she couldn't. "I also can't read my watch."

"My watch has a pearl face. I can track the time," Katherine said.

"Okay, twenty minutes, or sooner, if the truck stops," Leila told the captain.

"Just so you know, we have Phelps, Hopkins, and Annie Trent at the American outpost. Now we just need to get you home safe."

"That'd be nice," she agreed.

"Hang in there Leila," Evers said.

"We will."

Leila closed her eyes and said a prayer. Leila repeated back to Katherine what she'd discussed.

"Do you think it will work?" Katherine asked after Leila powered off the phone and handed it back to her.

"I wish I knew."

"That's why we've been taken and we're still alive. It's because you know something, right?"

Leila nodded. Then realized Katherine couldn't see it. "Yes. Yes, I do. Elijah works for the CIA. I used to, so besides doing translation, he sometimes asks me to come with him for a little more work. But nothing like this."

"You can't tell them what you know. It's the only leverage that you have," Katherine told her.

"I know."

"When I was approached to come to Syria, I was

suspicious. But they also knew that my family on my mother's side was Syrian. I'm sure that's why they approached me. I've been horrified at what I've seen, all the displaced and starving people because of al-Assad. Just growing some food would help."

Leila could hear Katherine working herself up into tears. She couldn't let that happen. If Katherine cried, she was worried that she'd start crying.

"How did you hide the phone?" Leila asked.

Katherine gave a hint of a chuckle. "The way women have been hiding things since they created a corset. My bra. No one wants to cop a feel of sixty-five-year-old breasts." This time, she chuckled, and so did Leila.

It helped. Laughing. If she weren't laughing, she'd be throwing up in the corner of the truck.

Suit Man knew that Leila had answers and the only reason that she could think of for bringing Katherine along with her was to use her to get Leila to answer questions. They'd hurt this nice woman to get Leila to tell them things. If she did, then four prisoners would not be released. They'd end up rotting in jail. *God knows what's happening to them.*

Then there would be the contact or contacts in al-Assad's government who'd likely be killed, and she couldn't forget about the man who was to deliver the diamonds.

Fuck!

She began to push her fingers through her hair and cried out in pain.

"What's wrong, Leila? Dammit, I didn't check your other cheek. I got caught up in the phone issue."

"No, it's not my cheek. I forgot he'd pulled me up by

my hair, and like a nitwit I tried to run my fingers through it like I always do."

"Got it."

There was silence in the truck. Leila didn't have it in her to make conversation. She was too upset over her realization that it was up to her to decide who got hurt or possibly killed. She should never have agreed to help Elijah out in the first place. It didn't matter if he was a good man and a friend of her father's. He was still CIA, and they played at the high roller table.

Stupid.

Stupid.

Stupid.

"Leila, they obviously questioned Elijah for information and didn't get it. Now they want to question you even further, right?"

"Yes," Leila answered slowly.

"Do you think they think I'm in on it?"

Leila considered lying, but they needed to be a solid team. "No, Katherine, I'm pretty sure they know you're not part of the CIA."

"So the only reason to take me with you is to use me. To hurt me. If they hurt me, they think you'll tell them what you know. Do I have that right?"

"You're smart. I guess that's why you're CEO of a large corporation."

"Founder. I'm a scientist at heart."

"I'll up that to really fucking smart."

"Are you protecting good people, Leila?" Katherine's voice trembled just a little. "Is it worth it?"

Leila reached out, fumbling until she touched and grabbed her hand. "They're good people. I promise you, they're good people."

"Then we can get through the ugly."

LINC SMELLED THE CIGARETTE SMOKE. He cut his eyes to the left and nodded as he saw Jase had noted the same thing. Jase pointed to another alley. And they were in luck. Two lines of laundry were gently swaying in the night breeze. It was two stories up, but not a problem. Linc even saw one of the hats that men wore, which would help him out because of his blond hair.

He climbed up a wall and pulled down three kaftans, none that would really fit Jase, but he'd just have to deal. He climbed up farther until he hit the roof, then pulled on the kaftan and the hat. Taqiyah? He wasn't really sure if that was what they were called.

From the four-story elevation, he had a better shot of finding some sort of vehicle. Using his night vision binoculars, he found three potential targets. He looked down and Jase gave him the all-clear signal, so he climbed back down and handed Jase his kaftan.

"You know this won't fit, right?"

"The other one is smaller." Linc grinned.

Jase left most of his gear on, but took off his rifle so that he could wear it outside of his kaftan. "I look like a sausage."

"Yep," Linc nodded. "Now, I've scoped out three possibilities. One actually looks like it can go faster than seven kilometers an hour."

"Let's get going."

Linc led the way. They avoided the small main street, instead sticking to the back alleys.

Linc held up his fist as he saw a red door on one of the

stone walls begin to open. An old woman stepped out and picked up a pail that had been beside the door, then went back inside. They continued on.

When they got to the truck, they found a problem. It was parked in the middle of a chicken coop. If they went in there to get it, they'd stir up the chickens and the household would come running.

"An unusual parking spot," Jase whispered.

"Cars are so valued in Syria that they will them to their children. They're going to protect them."

"Now you tell me. Why didn't we take the OKA?"

"Busted engine block?" Linc reminded him.

Linc tilted his head and Jase followed him as they melted down another alley. The next closest was a bright yellow taxi, an old Peugeot. When they got there, they found another problem. Two dogs were tied to the bumper.

"I guess car theft is common, huh?" Jase asked.

Linc shrugged.

They moved onto the last possible car that Linc had scoped out.

"My God, man, it's a fucking boat, not a car. What is it? A Buick from the fifties?" Jase whispered.

Linc pulled out his binoculars. "It's a Buick Riviera, and I have no idea when it was built. But you're right, it is a boat. It'll house a whole hell of a lot more people than that small little Nissan."

"This is going to be a problem," Jase said.

"Thanks, Captain Obvious."

They both looked at the four men sitting on overturned crates at a small table. They were playing cards. There was a kerosene lantern lighting up the table. All four of the men were armed. Like Linc and Jase, they had their automatic rifles strapped across their chests over their kaftans.

One of them threw down his cards and cackled. The obvious winner. Everybody threw in their cards, and one man gathered them and started shuffling.

Linc looked at his watch. They'd left Gideon an hour and ten minutes ago. They needed to get a move on. They needed a distraction, one that would preferably not cause loss of life. He looked over at Jase.

"I've got C-4," Jase said. "That'll distract them. Any ideas on how to deploy?"

Linc looked around. They were in the old part of the city that had taken many of the hits during the occupation by ISIS. Some buildings looked like empty shells, but he knew that could be deceiving. People could still use the buildings as shelter, especially as the nights were getting colder.

"Let's go look around."

As a sniper, Linc was used to shimmying up walls and buildings to get into the best positions to take a shot. A block away from the men playing cards, he found a fairly tall building to climb up to consider distraction options.

Half a block away, he saw an oil drum with simmering embers. Obviously, it was used for heat. It would be perfect. It was set against rubble that had once been some sort of building. The problem was, it was out in the open and no good way to approach without being seen, but that was Jase's specialty. Linc didn't know how such a big man could go unseen, but he'd watched in awe as he'd managed it, time and time again.

"Jase," he whispered softly into his mic.

"Yeah?"

"Around the corner to your right, then down the alley,

take another right. You'll see an oil drum with a small fire. Plant the C-4 there. Just a little, but enough to keep them occupied and enough to drown out the engine while we drive away. Once you do and you're clear, I'll shoot it. That should make a fine distraction."

Jase chuckled. "Well, that's clear as mud. Any chickens or dogs nearby?" Jase asked.

"Nope."

"On it."

Linc set up his rifle, using the ledge of the building to steady it. He took aim at the barrel and waited.

Six minutes later, he saw the walking sausage slip up to the oil can. Jase bent down as if to tie his shoe. Made sense in case he was spotted. From this angle Linc couldn't see Jase planting the C-4, but he knew he'd succeeded, because he stood back up. Then, like mist on water, he moved back to the alley.

Linc spotted the C-4. It looked like a lot.

Dammit.

He took the shot, and the oil can flew into to the sky as an explosion burst in a twenty-foot diameter.

Dammit.

He heard yelling. He turned his rifle to the car and saw the men running toward the explosion. Now was their chance.

He shimmied down the side of the building til it was safe to jump. He ran full out to the Buick, not caring if he was seen. He'd just be one more man in a kaftan running around because of the explosion.

Jase was in the driver's seat.

"No keys."

"Fuck," Linc responded.

Jase had his multi-tool knife out. "I'm on it," Jase

assured him. Linc watched as he pulled out the flathead screwdriver and jammed it into the ignition and turned. The car roared to life. Jase grinned.

"Nice job. Now get us the fuck out of here," Linc said.

"It was luck," Jase said. "Nothing but luck."

"Let's hope it lasts."

"THEY CAN TRACK US," Leila said as she hung up the phone with Captain Evers and shoved the phone back at Katherine. Leila prayed that the power on the phone would last long enough for them to pinpoint their whereabouts. She heard the rustling of clothing but couldn't see anything. Then the back of the truck doors were flung open and the moonlit sky illuminated the back.

"Get out of the truck," a man yelled in Arabic.

As soon as they stumbled to the back of the truck, someone grabbed each of them by one of their arms and yanked them out so that they fell to the ground. Leila didn't make a sound, and neither did Katherine.

Leila remained exactly where she was. On the ground was good, on the ground was great. Fresh air and nobody was hitting her.

She heard footsteps coming toward them. Then she saw wingtip shoes in front of her. "On your knees," he said in Arabic.

Leila didn't move.

"Do you really want me to let my guards hurt you? They will. As a matter of fact, they would be happy to."

Why did he have to sound so pleasant?

Leila slowly pushed up.

"What did he say?" Katherine asked.

"He wants us on our knees."

"For the record, I don't like this."

The man chuckled. "Katherine, there are a lot of things you will not like," he said in English.

Leila glanced over at her and she saw the woman shudder. But she kept her face impassive and got up onto her knees. So did Leila.

"It's occurred to me we really aren't in any real rush. Now, Captain Mousa," Suitman tipped his head to the man that Leila had previously considered the leader. "Mousa thinks we should do some intensive interrogation now, and he is disappointed with my decision. When you see what I have in store for you, I want you to thank me for my benevolence."

Suitman stopped talking. Leila knew this tactic. How many times had it been used on her during awkward things like interviews and dates? Be silent and wait for Leila to speak.

"What do you plan to do with us?" Katherine Cole asked.

Dammit.

Suitman grinned. "I'm glad you asked that, Mrs. Cole. Or should I call you doctor? I am sorry to be meeting you under such strained circumstances. I too was on track to get a degree in medicine. Let me introduce myself. My name is Vugar Gadirov. You have probably never heard of me. I attended university in the States. But when my father was killed, I came to my homeland to take over the family business."

"Katherine, I have read many good things about your company. You have made amazing strides in creating drought-resistant soybeans. This is something that Syria could definitely benefit from. It's too bad you're here under unlawful circumstances."

This time, Katherine said nothing.

Good.

"Time to get up off your knees now, ladies."

Leila squinted. She saw they were in the courtyard, in what looked like a hotel, but that couldn't be right.

"I see you're impressed with my home, Leila. You will be my guests for a few days. I'm afraid you will not like the accommodations that I have in store for you, but after a day or two, I think you will be more than happy to give me the answers I need."

Again he tipped his head, and men rushed behind her and Katherine. She was hauled up into a standing position. "Follow me," Vugar said in Arabic.

"Ow!"

Leila winced as she heard her friend's sharp outcry. She looked over at her and saw where two guards were practically dragging Katherine along, her arms forced behind her at odd angles.

They finally stopped in the middle of the courtyard.

"Here is fine," Suitman said. He turned to one of his men. "Get me the ladder."

Leila looked in front of her and saw a steel grate on the flagstone. She couldn't see what it was covering.

"Leila."

She looked up but said nothing.

How come the man always looks so calm? It's fucking spooky.

Two men who were behind the evil asshole came up and lifted the grate, and Leila looked down into a pit of darkness.

"I have the ladder, Sir."

"We have done you the courtesy of cleaning out the refuse from our last guests. But that is the only courtesy you will be extended until I get the answers I need."

Leila watched as the ladder that had to be twelve feet tall was lowered into the hole. Every hair on her body stood on end. She swallowed back a whimper that begged to be released. She couldn't bear to look at Katherine. What the hell had she gotten that woman into?

When the man had finished lowering the ladder, Vugar looked at the two men who were still holding Katherine. "Her first," he said.

"No," Leila argued. "Me first. If she falls and kills herself, your entire plan goes up in smoke. Let me go first and that way I can help her if she loses her balance."

He smiled slowly. "I don't know, Leila. Twenty-four hours of you down in that hole with a corpse would definitely get you to talk, don't you think?"

"No. I don't. I think it would make me more likely to find a way to slit my wrists. So let me go down the ladder first."

Even his laughter made her queasy.

"You are a delight. Fine, you can go first, then Katherine can go."

Leila took the four steps necessary to get to the ladder, then she backed down five rungs and waited for Katherine to follow her. It took them all of three minutes to get to the bottom of the dark and foul, smelly bottom. Every instinct she had was to grab the ladder and yank at it, causing whoever was pulling it back to be jerked over the edge of the hole, but that would only injure her and or Katherine.

The sound of the grill grinding over the tiles as it was pushed over the hole sickened her. Leila jumped. Had she heard something? No, it was just the sound of Katherine rubbing against the side of the hole as she leaned against it. She tried not to look down at her feet, so she closed her eyes. She didn't want to know if there were bugs or rats.

She just didn't want to know.

7

"AND WE CAN'T USE A BLACK HAWK. WHY AGAIN?" LINC asked.

"It's a dead issue. And besides that, I've got some more wonderful news. The al-Assad government has just said Al Tanf Outpost is shut down for the next forty-eight hours. So it's just us kids."

"Do we know why?" Linc asked.

"Just concentrate on driving," Kostya muttered.

"Yeah, you're going to get us killed. I always thought it was going to be a firefight, not because you decided to drive a sixty-year-old Buick like a ninety-year-old granny on meth," yelled Jase from the back as he gripped the headrest behind Linc.

"Gideon, this makes no sense. From the intel you've received, we're not heading toward ISIS or Al Qaeda strongholds. We're heading toward someone who is basically one of al-Assad's oligarchs."

"Not al-Assad's. This guy is all on his own. He's an arms dealer and information broker, and he's walking a very fine line. If any of the countries he's doing business with realizes he's getting and giving information to another, he's dead." Gideon explained. "He's in bed with governments in Azerbaijan, Georgia, Russia, Turkey, Belarus, and Syria. He's got so much money now he could buy a small country."

"And he lives around here?" Jase asked incredulously.

The man was right. The burnt-out shell of the city of Homs was a bitter sight to see.

"He has homes all around the world," Gideon answered, "including one in each country that he siphons money out of. Syria is one of those countries."

"So, what is it he wants from Leila and Katherine, or Elijah, for the matter?" Linc asked Gideon.

"If he's a player, this is an operation that is much bigger than something Jerry would run," Linc said. "Unless they just stumbled on something at the wrong place at the wrong time."

"Do you believe the report that we got from the CIA?" Jase asked, as Linc continued to drive down a small two-lane road like he was a Formula One driver.

"You mean the one that said that they were bringing in Landry and Cole to do business with al-Assad directly, and bypass USAID? No. Not buying it one bit. That was definitely a cover story for something bigger. This guy, Vugar Gadirov, he's too big of a player to be concerning himself with something like that."

"Not even for Landry Oil?" Linc asked.

Shit!

He swerved to miss the chunk of asphalt that was missing out of the road.

Would have fucked up the car for good.

"Nah, Landry Oil would be a nit on a gnat for this guy. However, I have Clint, Dex and Kane all digging deep on our boy Vugar and trying to see what drives him," Gideon explained.

"Good. Are we close?" Linc asked. The moon was bright, and he was beginning to see trees and there were walls that had been put back up on the side of the road. No graffiti. It looked like an area that had been cleaned up after all the fighting and the earthquake, and it was eerie, considering they'd just driven through Homs where it looked like Godzilla and Mothra had duked it out.

"About one klick, you should see some way to exit this highway—"

Jase laughed. "You're calling this a highway?"

"As I was saying," Gideon continued. "After about five hundred meters, you should see a right-hand exit. Take it. We're going to continue on for five klicks, then you two will go on foot the last five. His mansion slash compound is ten klicks, but he'll be heavily guarded. What the guys are feeding me is that he always goes around with an entourage, and he also avails himself to the local guns for hire."

"Sounds good," Linc said. "Why are you staying back with the Buick?" he asked Gideon.

"Want to see if Evers calls in with any more details."

"Got it." Linc turned to Jase. "You might win on the track on the base, but on ice, I'll beat you seven ways to Sunday."

"What are you talking about? This isn't ice. It's just a little cold," Jase bantered before he took off running.

"Need any help getting the car hidden?" Linc asked Gideon.

"Nah, I'm good. Better go catch him."

Linc bit his bottom lip, then gave a feral smile. "Guess so."

"NOPE, NOT WORKING," Leila said for the third time. "I can't get a signal. The rock walls of this fucking hole are making it impossible."

I want to throw the goddamned piece of shit against the wall!

"Satellites take a long time to move now that they're taking so many pictures." Katherine said. "Leila, do you know who this guy is?"

"Nope, but he doesn't seem the type who needs five million in diamonds. I get the feeling he has a much bigger reason than the diamonds. Five million would just be chump change to him."

"Yes, I got that same feeling," Katherine agreed.

"He knew a hell of a lot about me. It was like he was reading off my C.V."

"What's a C.V.?" Katherine asked.

"A resume. C.V. stands for Curriculum Vitae. I use that because I was trying to get a year of study in the E.U. But so far, no bites."

A giggle bubbled up. Then a chuckle. Then full-fledged laughter.

"Care to share with the class?" Katherine's executive voice made her laugh more. Leila reached out with one hand until she found a wall, then she leaned against.

"Stop that nonsense."

Leila tried her best not to burst out laughing at Katherine's last remark. She really did, but it burst out and she had to wipe the tears off with her sleeve. When she got herself under control, she reached out to Katherine.

"Grab my hand. You'll run into it if you're facing the

wall and you head toward my voice. I'm to the right of you." She felt Katherine's fingers touch hers. Leila stepped over and wrapped her arms around the older woman.

"I was laughing because it is wonderful that we were having a nice and normal conversation. Here we are, locked in this hole, with no actual idea if anybody knows where we are, and we will probably have to listen to Vulgar Vugar drone on."

"You're right, he seems like one of those Bond villains. Leila, do whatever you can to get him talking about himself and his evil master plan. Then we'll be rescued. Happens every time in the James Bond films."

Now Katherine was laughing.

Laughter.

Laughter equals joy.

Joy equals hope.

We'll make it.

Somehow.

Leila thanked God she'd been separated from Landry. There wouldn't be any laughter or hope with him. She would have found a ballpoint pen and jabbed it into his jugular by now.

"I've got an idea on how we can while away the time. Can you think of who at Langley might have ratted you and Elijah out?"

"It couldn't have been anyone who was in on the real reason we were there. We were reporting straight up to the highest level, the director. Can't get any higher than that in the CIA. Anybody higher is just a Washington hack who doesn't know what's going on."

"So, there were no middlemen between Elijah and the director?" Leila heard the doubt in Katherine's voice.

"This was a top-secret op. Elijah reported directly to

the first assistant director, and his boss is the director. He bypassed every step in between. I'd been amazed when Elijah told me he'd skipped all those levels to talk to the director. That was unheard of. It would have to be the director or the first assistant director who is the leak."

"Or the person typing up the notes or filing the files. It just takes one person to tell and then the entire mission falls apart. Then there is the fact that somebody sold the information for money," Katherine pointed out.

"You're right, Katherine."

"Any ideas?" she asked Leila.

"I would put my life on the line that it wasn't the two higher ups that Elijah was talking to. Elijah is too smart to be fooled."

"Okay, then it's my thought, it's somebody else who read this information, and would have to send Elijah to buy four American prisoners."

Leila shook her head in the dark. Then spoke aloud so that Katherine could hear. "I doubt Vugar would care about America paying for prisoners. I also don't think that he wants the diamonds. There has to be something more." Leila stopped talking. "I can't think of anything. Can you?"

"You're going to have to tell me where the diamonds are one more time, and how Elijah was going to contact the man."

Leila started explaining once more.

LINC SQUINTED as the sun started to come up over the horizon.

Fuck. Fuck. Fuck.

"We're screwed," Jase whispered.

"Yep."

"Our comm system is close enough to Gideon so we don't have to use our phones," Jase continued to whisper to Linc.

"Yes, they are," Gideon said sarcastically. "You've had your mic on for the last thirty seconds, ever since you and Linc stopped. Not good."

Jase winced.

"Now, why are you screwed? Aw shit, now I see the sun's coming up. Are you going to wait?" Gideon asked in a low voice.

"We don't have a choice. We're a hundred meters away from the fence surrounding the place," Linc said softly.

"And I've counted five different guards patrolling, all with AK-47s, all with grenade launchers, same as us."

"I guess when you have billions, you can afford to set your team up with all the bells and whistles," Gideon whispered.

"Which just might mean he had someone good training them," Linc whispered.

"There's Mr. Pessimistic," Jase grinned. "I've missed you."

Linc gave Jase the finger, then he pulled out his phone.

"According to the last coordinates we had for her, we are exactly in the right place."

"We're waiting, Gideon. If you get any intel in the meantime, send it our way. Is your hiding place any good?" Jase asked.

"As good as we could make it and possibly get back out when you find the women."

"Gotcha," Jase said.

They'd gotten rid of their kaftans as soon as they were clear of the city of Homs. Their desert camouflage would give them cover during the day, as long as they could fade into the low-lying brush.

Linc saw the gathering storm clouds and knew that they would be in for a rainy day of hiding. He pulled out his poncho and Jase did the same thing.

"Oh joy," Linc muttered.

RAIN FELL through the grate onto Leila and Katherine.

I'm going to see this as a positive.

I'm going to think positive thoughts.

I will.

Rainbows.

Unicorns.

Bullshit.

"Is your bra lace?" Katherine asked. "Or is it more substantial?"

"What? What are you talking about?"

"I'm thirsty as hell, and it would be lovely if we had something more to drink out of than just our hands."

"Yeah. Yeah, it's a sports bra. It'd work." Leila chuckled. "I will no longer bitch about being a size D cup again." She unbuttoned her blouse and unhooked her bra and handed it to Katherine.

"No, it's best if we both do it. You hold one side, I'll hold the other side taut. That way we should be able to fill it the best."

"Whatever you say, you're the scientist."

The water was freezing cold, and goo from the grate was also being washed into the bra cups.

"There. That's enough. Drink, Leila," Katherine encouraged by nodding her head. Leila drank all the water from one cup. Then she drank only half the water from the second.

"You need to drink it all," Katherine encouraged. "We're both dehydrated."

"No, that's all right," Leila demurred.

"Are you worried that you might have to tinkle? You're among friends. I know I'm going to have to tinkle, because I intend to drink a lot of water."

Leila gave a bit of a laugh. After all, what else could she do?

"I enjoy hearing you laugh, Leila. Now drink up."

The cups had filled up with more rainwater, so she had to drink even more. She finished it all. They repeated the process for Katherine. Then, an hour later, when they both had to pee, Leila wasn't as embarrassed as she thought she'd be.

"I'm sorry Landry's dead," she said to Katherine. "But it would be hell stuck in a hole with him."

Katherine burst out laughing. "He'd be whining about this rain, that's for sure. But he'd love your look. It's like you're in a wet t-shirt contest."

Leila looked down at herself and grimaced. She didn't want Suitman to see her like this.

"Ahhh, I'm sorry, Leila. I wasn't thinking."

"It's okay, Katherine. This is what we agreed on. Sunshine, unicorns, and rainbows. We weren't going to let this get us down. Remember?"

"Actually, I'm not so sure that's going to work for me any longer," Katherine admitted. "My sciatic nerve hasn't liked everything we've done in the past twenty-four hours. I'm not going to be able to stand anymore."

"Here, let me help you," Leila said as she guided Katherine into a sitting position with both of her legs stretched out. She was letting out small whimpers of pain. Leila knew how excruciating it could be. Her grandfather suffered from this, and not even the shots they gave him would help. It took steroids, narcotics, and time to help him through the worst of it.

"Katherine, is there anything I can do for you?"

"No, sweetheart, I just have to ride it out. It's the same thing I have to do if I were back home in Boston."

"Yeah, but you wouldn't be sitting in three inches of pee and rainwater."

"Speaking of that, can you pass me the bra? I'm thirsty."

So spunky. There is no way her *nene* could have handled this. There would be tears and recrimination, but Leila would have had to hold strong.

"You wanna try singing? That usually cheers me up," Katherine suggested. "Plus, it always put my children in better moods during family road trips. Wanna try?"

"Sure," Leila said. She would have said yes to almost anything at this point.

"Okay, let's go with an old favorite, shall we?"

Katherine started to sing.

SHE'LL BE COMING round the mountain when she comes.

She'll be coming round the mountain when she comes.

She'll be coming round the mountain.

She'll be coming round the mountain.

She'll be coming round the mountain when she comes.

. . .

SHE'LL BE DRIVING six white horses, when she comes.

She'll be driving six white horses, when she comes.

She'll be driving six white horses, when—

"STOP! Please stop! You and Suitman win. I'll tell him everything. Anything he wants to know, I'll tell him. Just quit singing that song," Leila begged.

"Yeah, it is really more fun when you sing it in harmony. Are you an alto?"

"Katherine, are you really trying to torture me?"

Katherine laughed.

"You should see your face. For the last five minutes, I didn't notice the pain in my leg."

They both looked up as they heard the scratching up above. Then a clang as someone lifted the grate from over the hole. Neither of them made a sound.

"Hello, ladies. I do hope you enjoyed your accommodations."

This time, he was wearing a tan suit with a blue tie. Someone was holding an umbrella over him. Once again, Leila had the feeling his clothes were tailor-made for him.

"I want to make very clear what I require from you. There is somebody in al-Assad's organization who is a traitor. I want to meet this person and do business with him. You were going to, and I just want his information so that I might do a little business with him as well. Is that so bad?"

Again, Leila and Katherine didn't make a sound.

He turned around and spoke in Arabic. Leila could not make it out, because he was turned away from her. When he turned back with a flashlight, she figured that was what he had asked for.

"Ahh, I see the rain has been both a blessing and a curse. You've been able to drink some water, but if my nose doesn't deceive me, Katherine is now sitting in a brew of rainwater and piss. That must be delightful, dear."

Leila looked down at her friend and saw that she was gritting her teeth so tight that she might break her back molars.

"I also see that the rain and rainwater have done wonders for your nipples, Leila. They are very enticing. Perhaps I will not just kill you after you provide me with the information. Perhaps I will keep you in my bed. For a while, at least. It is so fun to break a woman.

"Well, it's time for your next twenty-four hours. There's no rain in the forecast. So pretty soon you're going to have to start drinking that swirl of rainwater, piss, and Allah only knows what else is down on that floor, so you can stay alive."

He told his men to put the grate back over the hole.

Leila could hear his laughter as he walked away.

"How can I feel despair and fury at the same time, Katherine?"

"Hold on to the fury, Leila. You're going to need it."

8

IT WAS THE SECOND THROAT HE'D SLIT THAT NIGHT. FOR A brief second Linc knew that this might haunt him—as would all the others—but right now, he was a SEAL and he had a job to do.

"Number two down," he whispered into his mic. "I'm continuing around the perimeter clockwise."

"Mine are dead. I'm going counterclockwise," Jase said.

"Jase, I have one right inside the gate, checking the perimeter."

"Me too."

"No noise, children." Gideon reminded them.

"Yes, Dad," Jase whined.

"Knives," Linc said into his mic.

"Agreed."

"We're going to need to synchronize. I'll count down."

"Five.

"Four.

"Three.

"Two.

"Now!"

Linc let go of his knife and it hit his target perfectly. With that much force, not only did he hit the man's jugular, but he also damn near cut off his head. He was dead by the time he hit the ground. Another silent kill. He heard nothing from Jase's side, but he was aways away. How big was this damned house, anyway? Just how much space did one man need?

"Got him," Jase whispered.

"Me too," Linc whispered.

At least there wasn't a guard tower. "I'm going to keep going," Linc said.

"Same."

Linc finished his patrol at the back section of the mansion. They'd started at the front, where the driveway turned into a courtyard. There had been three Humvees, a truck, and a Mercedes parked in the front. God knew how many were parked in the four-bay garage he had seen.

"Did you see any more guards," Linc asked Jase as he met him.

"No, but I did see two lights on, in what looked like a big room on the third floor, on the east side."

Linc looked down at his watch. It was oh two fifteen.

"Did you see any activity?" Linc asked.

"Negative," Jase answered.

"More than likely, that's our target," Gideon whispered into their ears.

"Agreed," Linc said. "From what we saw during the day, they change guard shifts every four hours. We've got three hours and forty-five minutes before the shift."

"We took down six guards. We know there are six more. That would fit the three Humvees," Jase said. "That looked to me like an armored Mercedes, so let's say four in that."

"One of them would have been Vugar," Gideon pointed out.

"You're right," Linc agreed. "So, at the minimum, ten guards, when you count the driver of the truck, Vugar, and two hostages."

"I don't see any cameras, do you?" Jase asked. He had his binoculars up and was checking out the back of the mansion. "There aren't even any security lights."

"He probably just depends on muscle and the fact that it's Syria. He probably thinks no one will take a shot at him, here," Linc said as he looked over the backyard and the house through the scope of his sniper rifle.

"I see something," he whispered. "I can see the kitchen," he continued to speak softly. "Someone just opened the refrigerator. He's just wearing boxers."

"Can you track him to see where in the house he goes after he has his glass of milk?" Jase asked. "After all, it does a body good."

"Cut the shit, Jase," Gideon said. "We don't have time. Linc, you're wrong to think you have til the next guard change. You want to get out of there with the hostages, without them knowing, then get them to me and all of us getting out of here before they even know what happened."

What's more, the longer Leila and Katherine were in the hands of Vugar, the worse it was for them. God knew what was happening to them.

"Let's get over the fence, and each of us go to the back of the house. You take the east, and I'll take the west."

Jase nodded.

It was a ten-foot-high steel fence with spikes on top. Both he and Jase cleared it in less than a minute.

Linc shook his head. The lack of security was amazing compared to some places they'd encountered in the past. Both of them crouched and ran to their respective corners, their rifles up. There was ornamental shrubbery growing against the house—another big no-no—and Linc used it to hide himself as he peered in the different ground-floor windows.

"Got it," Jase spoke into his ear. "Bunk beds, four men."

"Asleep?" Linc asked.

"Affirmative."

"Stay with them. I want to check out the lit room. See if it's Vugar's room."

Linc carefully eased around the east corner of the concrete mansion when he immediately found a window. He peeked in. Bunk beds set up for four men. Two of the beds were occupied.

"I've got two more guards accounted for," Linc said into his mic.

Linc stepped back four feet from the house and looked upward. The lights were on. He saw shadows against the curtains. It was easy to tell that it was a man and a woman. For a split second, his heart dropped. Then he smiled.

"Vugar has a woman with him. The way she's wound around him, I'd say she's willing, so not Katherine or Leila," Linc whispered into his mic.

The man was occupied. He couldn't hope for anything better.

"Last resort is questioning him. Try to find the women and get the fuck out of there without being noticed." Gideon said.

"Thanks for pointing out the obvious," Jase responded.

Linc rolled his neck, then went back to checking for cameras and peeking into every window that he could. He had to stop when he got to the courtyard. It was covered in flagstone and was used more as a parking area. There were no bushes in the front, just some tall cypress trees that were planted beside the courtyard.

"Jase, I'm going to check out the windows up front. I can do the climbing. Check out to see if there are any keys in the Humvees."

"Gotcha." Linc heard the smile in his teammate's voice. They were on the same page. If they could find a set of keys, they could use one of the Humvees to get the fuck out of here. All it would take would be for them to take out the other vehicles so they couldn't follow. It was possible.

"Found one," Jase whispered, as Linc was looking into the third-floor front window. He saw a hallway with a man in front of a door. He was almost asleep. Obviously, he was guarding Vugar's bedroom door. No hostages there.

He continued to move sideways across the front of the building and ended up on one of the balconies. He looked in, hoping that maybe he would find Leila and Katherine. What he found was a guard who was smoking weed.

"I found one to question," Linc said into his mic. "In the room with the balcony."

He slid in through the balcony's French doors. The guard didn't even notice. Linc took out his all-purpose tool and flipped open the small knife. It would have to do.

He went up behind the guard and gripped him around his neck. He pointed the knife just under his eye, pushing in so that he could feel the tip.

"Jase, he's in the mood to talk. Where are you?"

"I'm here."

Linc turned around a little with the guard still in his arms. "Nice move, Linc." His words came out like he'd eaten rocks for breakfast.

Then Jase took out his own all-purpose tool and pulled out the small knife. He made quick work of the man's pants and jerked them down to his ankles. He pressed the knife against his scrotum.

Both he and Jase were silent for a while. Then the man started to cry. He started to whisper words.

Jase held up his hand. He started talking. It was obvious he was asking questions. The man kept shaking his head. Jase's knife pushed in and blood dripped to the floor. The man was sobbing. A spate of Arabic came out of his mouth. Jase took away the knife and smiled.

"Knock him out, Linc. With the weed and his bleeding balls, he should be out for hours."

Linc hit the guard in his temple and he fell to the ground. They both made quick work of tying him up and shoving a doily they found on a fancy-assed chair into his mouth.

"We need to go out the same way we came in. The women are outside," Jase said.

"Outside?"

"There's a hole in the middle of the courtyard. It's covered by a grate. They're in there."

"What are you talking about?" Linc wanted to know.

"Apparently there is some kind of hole cut into the flagstone that Vugar puts people in when he's pissed at them. He does it to guards that fuck up. Now he has two women in there."

Jase and Linc went to the balcony and crouched down

so that could view the courtyard. They used their binoculars so that they could pinpoint where the grate was.

"Found it," Linc said as he pointed.

It wasn't near anything. It was away from the gate, the staircase to the entry, and the garage. Instead, it was near what Linc thought might be a path that would lead to the shed that he had seen on his trip around the house.

"There's a lot of cover to get to them," Jase said.

Linc nodded as he eyed the tall cypress trees.

He looked over his shoulder at the guard. The fact that he had a part in putting these two women in a hole made his mind want to explode.

"Linc, hold it together. We'll get them out."

Jase was a friend. He knew that when women were hurt, it was a hot button for Linc.

"Are you going to be okay climbing down?" Linc asked.

"Hell yeah. You're not the only hotshot. Let's move," he whispered.

They were soon on the ground and keeping to the wall, then along the line of cypress trees along the east side of the courtyard. They stopped when the path to the shed started. Beyond that, Linc could see the grate.

Goddammit, it had been raining most of the day. They couldn't be in there, could they?

Why couldn't it rain now? It would be great cover for them. Linc lifted his fist, and Jase halted. Linc crawled up to the grate and looked down. He couldn't see anything. It was dark. He tilted on his night vision goggles. His stomach dropped.

One woman was on her knees, with the other woman's head and shoulders in her lap. Then he heard it. Someone was humming. He recognized the song. It was *YMCA*. His lip tipped upward. *Good for them.*

He backed up and turned to Jase. In the lowest whisper possible, he spoke. "We've got to have an exit plan before we get to them. Katherine's passed out. Leila seems to be okay."

Jase nodded. "I've been thinking. It'll take too long for us to shoot out the tires of each vehicle. They'd get us before we're done. The Humvee with the keys is set up just right to leave the courtyard. Nothing in front of it, so we're good. We just need to disable the other cars."

"If you're thinking of disconnecting the spark plugs —"

"Give me some credit. We need to disable everything at the same time."

"Did you bring enough C-4 for this?" Linc asked.

"Depending where I place it, and how good of a shot you are, everything should be fine. Plus, I got a remote to open the gate out of the Mercedes."

"Okay, let's see about the women."

Linc dropped to the ground and crawled on his elbows and shins to get to the grate. He looked down again, using his goggles.

"Stay quiet," Linc said in a voice that would only carry down the hole. "We're here to rescue you."

The one woman didn't move. The other woman, the one who was kneeling, looked up at him. It was Leila.

"Leila, we'll get you out of here."

"Who are you?"

"United States Navy."

Linc moved to the other side of the grate. Then he and Jase lifted the heavy metal so that they could get the two women out of a literal hellhole.

"You're going to need a ladder," Leila whispered. "I know there's one close by. When Vugar asked for it, one of his men could get it quickly."

That was what he remembered. She was calm, and she was smart. "It'll be in the shed," he said to Jase. "I'll get it."

Linc stood up as soon as he was past the line of sight of the house. It wasn't far, and he found the ladder leaning up against the shed. Apparently, it got a lot of use. He hauled it back, and as he got close, he crouched down again.

With his night vision goggles still on, he lowered the ladder carefully so it didn't hit either of the two women.

"Katherine won't be able to make it. Can you carry her up?"

"You climb up first, then that will make room for me to climb down and lift her."

"I can't. If I let her go, her head will go underwater."

Holy mother of God.

"Jase, I'll get her up a few rungs, then you can pull her up," Linc said as he started down the ladder.

"Right," Jase replied.

When Linc stepped down onto the floor of the hole, the water went past the top of his boot. It smelled.

"You can let go of Katherine now. I've got her," Linc said.

He put her over his shoulder and started up the rungs of the ladder. Jase grabbed her before Linc even made it to the top.

"I've got her," Jase assured him.

He turned around to get Leila and found her already halfway up the ladder. He went with it and turned back and got out of the hole. When he was out, he held out his hand, and Leila took it. He helped to lift her the rest of the way out of the hole.

Once she was steady on her feet, she wrapped her arms around him.

"Thank you. Oh, my God. Thank you."

9

JASE WAS DRIVING. THEY STARTED OUT SLOW AND STEADY. First he hit the remote and when the gate opened, he smoothly drove out. The plan was to haul ass until they were out of range of normal automatic rifles and grenade launchers, then leave it to Linc to do what he did best.

Jase had left the compound's gate open for Linc. With his scope, he could clearly see the interior of the courtyard. One of the Humvees was starting to move. Before he hit that one, he wanted to hit the garage, in case there were other vehicles he didn't know about.

He saw the C-4. Jase had marked it with the orange glow in the dark paint stick. Linc took the shot. He started to line up his next shot. It was the Mercedes at the back of the courtyard. Then he saw the explosion out of the corner of his eye.

Bullseye.

Again, Jase had marked the target for him. Linc hoped like hell that Jase was right, and that he'd placed the C-4 next to the gas tank, because that Mercedes was built like a tank. Linc took the shot, then changed his focus to the lead Humvee coming his way. They were probably eleven hundred meters out. It entered his consciousness for a split second that the Mercedes had blown.

Now it was the Humvee's turn.

Fuck.

He couldn't see the markings. He should have shot them first. Jase had probably placed the C-4 on the side of the vehicle. Now they were a thousand meters out. He could see the passenger side had his rifle out. Linc set his eye to his rifle and shot the driver. Then he shot the man in the passenger seat. He watched dispassionately as the Humvee careened off the dirt road, into a tree.

The next Humvee appeared out of the dust of the first Humvee. Now it was maybe five hundred meters out. Linc set up his shot for the driver when out of the corner of his eye he saw orange. He grinned.

Linc repositioned his rifle and fired. This close, he didn't have to wait long at all. He watched as the front of the Humvee blew upwards by at least five feet before coming back down. Smoke was coming out of the engine, but nobody was getting out. Then the engine blew. Linc picked up his rifle and got back into the passenger seat.

"Time to go."

He slammed his door shut, put on his seat belt, then turned to look in the back seat. "What's wrong with her, Leila?"

"She thought it was her sciatica acting up. She was in terrible pain. I think that was about noon yesterday. She passed out before the sun went down today. She convulsed once. I thought she was going to die."

"Does she have a fever?" Jase asked.

"No."

"But you haven't been able to wake her up, is that right?" Linc asked.

"No, I haven't."

"We'll try to get her to a hospital as fast as we can," Linc promised as their vehicle slowed down.

"Why are we stopping?" Leila wanted to know.

"There's one more member of our team."

"I know you, don't I?" Leila stared hard at Linc's face. "You were in Turkey. In Batman when we were working on that situation with Damla Akbas." Leila twisted her neck so she could look at Jase. "And you were there too."

"Good to see you again, Ms. Cloud. Sorry we couldn't get to you sooner," Jase said as he brought the Humvee to a halt.

LEILA FELT like Alice must have after she fell down the rabbit hole. That seemed like the best comparison, all things considered. How was it the same men she had worked with over a year ago were now in Syria saving her ass?

Does it matter?

Katherine moaned and Leila cringed. She hated what things had come to, and all because she agreed to work with Elijah, and she hadn't given Vugar the information he wanted.

The right back door opened and another man from Turkey got into the car. Gideon. He nodded at her. He shoved what looked like a computer tablet underneath his body armor and threw two white kaftans up at Linc, then he turned to her. "How are you doing, Leila?"

"Better now. I'm worried about Katherine."

"I see you have her laid out on the console," Gideon said, referring to the wide flat space between the driver and passenger seat that extended back between the two backseats. "Can you tell me what her status is?"

"She's been unconscious for five hours." Leila had checked the time on Katherine's watch when she'd finally passed out. "I told Linc," she looked back up to the passenger seat, "that's you underneath all that mud, isn't it?"

"Yeah, I'm Lincoln Hart, and the driver is Jase Drakos."

"And I'm Gideon. I'm thinking you remembered me since I'm not covered in mud," he teased.

Leila gave a short laugh and nodded. Then she turned her attention back to Katherine. "Are you a medic?"

"No, none of us are, but we have had basic medic training. Tell us what's happened." Gideon had his fingers to Katherine's neck, looking at his watch. He was obviously checking her pulse.

"Yesterday, at about noon, she developed excruciating pain from her sciatic nerve. We'd been standing up since we'd been put in the hole. We would lean against the wall and each other. It was too filthy to sit down."

Gideon moved from Katherine's head and sat back down in his seat.

"How's her pulse?" Leila asked.

"Low and thready. I got forty-five beats per minute. I took it twice."

"After her pain started, then what happened?" Gideon asked.

"She had to kind of lie down. There wasn't much room, so she sat down and stretched her legs. The pain got steadily worse, and I tried massaging her thigh. That helped for a little bit, then it started to make things worse."

"Understood. There isn't much you can do without medicine," Gideon said.

"When it got dark, her body started jerking. She couldn't control it. It wasn't a stroke. She was still talking, but she'd have involuntary jerks. Then one was so bad she passed out. But the jerks continued, and one seemed like a true convulsion. No, I mean it *was* a true convulsion. What little saliva she did have bubbled out of her mouth. By that time, the rain had stopped, and she was slumped over. There was so much water in the hole that I had to crouch down and put her head in my lap. I'm not sure how long that was. The next thing I knew, I heard Linc calling down to me."

Gideon nodded. "We'll get you both to safety."

"Guys, pull over and put on the robes. According to Rankin over at the base, the al-Assad government is for real about this shutdown. Humvees are normal, but not driven by muddy Americans."

Jase stopped the Humvee and yanked the bigger kaftan out of Linc's hand. "This time, *you* can look like a sausage." They both shimmied into the robes, then Jase got to driving.

IT TOOK ABOUT twenty minutes for Leila to go to sleep. Linc twisted his head to look back at her. She looked nothing like the buttoned-up professional he'd met in Turkey, but she was just as gorgeous. Maybe even more gorgeous, knowing a little bit of what she'd gone through and she kept her head and didn't give up.

"She's out," Linc whispered. "Who have you been in contact with?" he asked Gideon.

"Captain Evers. He's the liaison with the CIA dicks. So, he's getting the bullshit information."

"Why do we want that?" Linc asked.

"I relay it to the others back home, and it helps them see how the CIA is trying to fix Leila's phone."

"You mean that shitty piece of metal that did nothing for her? *That* phone?"

Linc didn't raise his voice, but the raw anger was palpable.

"Yeah, that phone."

"She must still have it with her, but I didn't think to ask for it."

"And I'm not about to grope her while she's sleeping to find it," Gideon said. He leaned over. "Leila." Nothing. He tapped her shoulder and said her name a little louder. "Leila, can you wake up for just a moment?"

Her big brown eyes opened. "Hmmm?" Then she focused on Gideon. Her brow furled. "Katherine?"

"No. You still have your phone, don't you?"

"You mean that piece of crap that didn't do a damn thing? That phone?"

Linc grinned. She thought the same way he did.

"Yeah, that phone," Gideon agreed. "Do you have it?"

"Katherine does. She's been keeping it in her bra." Leila leaned forward and tried to unbutton the top of her blouse, but it wasn't working. Linc realized it was because the blouse was too wet.

Linc took out his multi-purpose tool and pulled out his knife. "Here, use this. Or I could do it, and it would be easier."

It would definitely be safer if he did it. The rocking

Humvee that they were in would make it difficult for her to use the knife safely.

"Yes, you do it. Just undo the buttons until you get to the top of her bra. I'll fish out the phone after that."

"Got it."

She was so tired and shaky he was going to cut the fabric, whether she agreed to him doing it or not. He sliced through the buttons and pulled back the fabric. Just enough to expose the top part of Katherine's bra.

Linc watched as Leila pulled back the cup of the woman's bra, then he turned his head. "You can turn around again. I've got it."

"I want it." Gideon held out his hand. "If I can make this piece of shit work, we might be able to use this to our advantage," he said.

Leila sat back in the seat, and Linc saw her eyelids flutter down.

"Gideon, why would we need the phone to work? Aren't we just headed to the Al Tanf Outpost?"

"Yeah, but you never know."

10

IT WAS HOURS BEFORE THE DEBRIEF ENDED. FIRST, HE HAD to tell his story to Kostya, then there was the Skype call with that jerk Jerry Earnst. At least Kostya sat in on that one, so he could move things along when *Good Ole Jer* started asking irrelevant questions. What was the most frustrating aspect was the man's lack of interest in Vugar Gadirov. Now that was someone they needed to stop. When Jerry was wrapping up the debrief, Linc had had enough.

"So, Jerry?" he asked. He saw the man wince. He definitely wanted to be called Agent Earnst. Well, fuck that.

"Yes?"

"Don't you want more details about Vugar?"

"You described his house and his guards. Did you have any more relevant information?"

Linc thought about it and had to admit to himself, he didn't.

"There's the fact that he purposely kidnapped Leila

and Katherine and left them in a hole so they would provide him information."

Jerry smirked. "Yes, yes. I got all of that relevant information from Ms. Cloud. I have to go now. Thank you for your cooperation in this debrief."

The screen went blank.

"Do you believe that shit?" Linc asked Kostya.

"I got the same thing," Kostya said. "Thanks for your cooperation, but no thanks for rescuing their people. He's not what you would call a people person," Kostya chuckled.

"How's Katherine doing?" Linc asked.

"We're going to go check on her right now."

Linc followed Kostya out of the conference room. They walked down a hallway and turned, walked down another hall and turned, then walked down another. The place was like an ant farm. Finally, they reached a door that said medical on it. He opened it and there was a petty officer at a desk. He stood up and saluted Kostya.

"Sir, how can I help you?"

"We'd like to sign in to visit a couple of your new civilian patients. Katherine Cole and Elijah Hopkins."

"Please sign in here," the petty officer said as he indicated a login book with a pen on top. Kostya signed in first, then Linc did.

"You will find the men just as you go in. In the back behind the curtains is the woman's area."

"Thank you, Petty Officer Hawley."

When they turned the corner to the ward, they saw that there was space for twenty patients. The men's area had more beds occupied than Linc expected. It was easy to spot Elijah because he was over fifty, and all the other patients were barely over thirty. There was a nurse doing something with one of the IVs.

"How is he doing?" Kostya asked.

"Better. He's still in a coma, but the doctor ordered it."

"What's his prognosis?" Kostya asked.

"That's a question for his doctor. He should be available in fifteen or twenty minutes."

Kostya looked over at Linc. Both of them hoped for good news.

"We were hoping to check on Katherine Cole. Is it okay if we went into the women's section?" Kostya asked.

"I'll escort you," the nurse answered.

As they got closer to the curtain, they heard giggling. "That is the funniest song in the world. I can't believe I never heard it before."

It sounded like Leila talking, but her voice was a little garbled.

"How does the song go again?"

"She'll be riding on six white horses, coming round the mountain here she comes.

"She'll be on some horses, coming round the mountain. There she goes.

"There she goes again.

"She'll—"

"Ms. Cloud," a man's voice interrupted the song. "The anesthesia should wear off in an hour or so. You're going to be very sore. I need you to keep this ice pack on your face for fifteen minutes every hour. Can you do that?"

"Sure," she giggled.

"I've also prescribed something for the pain. The nurse will get your script filled and bring it to you."

"You got it, Doc. You're fabulous. My cheek doesn't hurt anymore, and it feels like I'm flying, so you did good." She giggled again.

Then she started to sing. "R, E, S, T, C, Respect. Find out what it means to you." It sounded like Leila, but he'd never heard her giggle or sing. Come to think of it, he'd never really seen her smile. But serious, stoic, kick-ass, he'd seen that often. Now, with her giggling, he couldn't help but chuckle. The nurse peeked around the corner then looked back at Linc and Kostya.

"It's fine to go in."

She pulled back the curtain wide enough for them to walk through. Sitting sideways on a bed was Leila. She was wearing hospital scrubs and in the bed next to her was Katherine Cole.

For just a moment Linc let himself remember how she looked in that wet blouse. She'd been breathtaking.

Shut it down. Focus on the now.

He looked over at Katherine. She was connected to IVs, but she was sitting up, and looking better than the last time Linc had seen her.

"Hi, Linc!"

"Hi, other hot guy!" Leila squealed.

Leila had a bandage around her face, with ice clearly placed against her cheek.

"Remember to only keep the ice on for fifteen minutes every hour, then again."

"I'm going to remember, nice doctor."

"Okay, I'm going to check on some of my other patients. You be good."

"I'm not promising anything." Leila laughed.

She twisted on the bed so she could see Katherine. "Wanna sing *YMCA*? We sang that in the hole while you were asleep. I couldn't do all the moves cause you were in my lap, but now I can."

Before she started, Linc quickly went to stand right in front of her. "Can we talk instead of sing?"

Leila looked confused, but then her expression brightened. "I really wanted to talk to you when we were in Turkey, but I had to leave for the States. Sometimes I get tangled up in things, you know?"

"I caught on to that." Linc smiled.

"I thought about you when I got back to the States. You were the prettiest of all the SEALs." She turned to Kostya. "Sorry, hot guy."

Katherine laughed from her bed, as Kostya grinned. "I think I can handle not being the prettiest."

Linc bowed his head. He just knew he was going to get a ration of shit from the guys for months. There was no way that Kostya wouldn't share what Leila had just said.

Linc looked up. "You're the beautiful one," Linc said. She held out her hands, and he took them in his. "What did the doctor say about your cheek?"

"My cheekbone broke. He made me sleep so he could reset it. I'll be fine, eventually. Oh yeah, I'm not beautiful. I went to the bathroom and looked in the sink mirror. I have two black eyes, and my hair is ratty. I don't look so good, but most of the time I look okay. Not beautiful, but okay. I'm a solid six on a scale of one to ten. I have good legs."

Kostya snickered.

Linc did his best not to laugh.

A six my ass.

"Come closer," Leila said as she pulled on his hands to draw him near. "I've got a secret."

He gave Kostya a helpless glance. His lieutenant just shrugged.

Linc rested his thighs against the hospital bed, beside her legs. "Okay, what is your secret?" he asked.

"They don't make it easy to find you. I tried asking for you when I was back home, but I couldn't. Sad. It was sad. I was sad."

Linc pulled his head away from her lips and looked down at her. "I looked for you, too. I was hoping you would be in Turkey or D.C., but you weren't."

"No, I was in France on a job. It was long-term, so I sublet my apartment. Were you sad, Linc? Were you sad like I was, that you couldn't find me?"

"Yes, Leila, I was sad."

"Leila, I've been timing your icepack," Katherine said. "It's been fifteen minutes."

"What?"

"You can take off your ice pack," Linc said softly.

He reached up to her face and helped her with the elastic band that held the ice pack in place. He winced when he saw just how bruised her cheek was. He'd always noted the swelling, but, with her light brown skin, it hadn't been as noticeable. But up close, Linc could clearly see the bruising.

"Thanks for your help," Leila said, then smiled and winced. "I wonder if the wonderful drugs are wearing off. He told me that aligning the bones together was going to hurt, that's why he kind of put me under. Then he said it would hurt for a few days afterward. But this level of pain is ridiculous."

She looked over at Katherine and smiled. "We can

bitch about being in pain now. We're not in the hands of Suitman."

She was sounding a little bit more sober.

"Ladies," Kostya interrupted. "Have you both had a chance to speak to Agent Earnst with the CIA?"

"I did," Leila said. "He reminds me of every manager I'd ever met at CIA Headquarters. He has the personality and brains of a potato. Why they put paper-pushers in charge, boggles the mind."

"My team knows about the diamonds, and the prisoner exchange, but Linc and I, and the others, are having a hard time wrapping our head around the idea that Vugar Gadirov went to the trouble of killing and kidnapping American civilians just for five million in diamonds."

"So do I." Leila said.

"Me too," Katherine said from her bed.

"But Agent Eager Scout didn't agree with my hypothesis that Vugar was up to something bigger."

Kostya rubbed the back of his neck. "My people have put together quite a file on Vugar, and there is not a chance in hell that he risked the kidnapping and killing of Americans for a five-million-dollar payday."

"Well, I don't know what I can do about it. This is an Elijah thing. Seriously, I was brought in as a translator and to help smooth things with Katherine and Robert Landry if they thought the cover project wasn't on the level."

"If that's true, how did you find out about the diamonds? Why did CIA Headquarters set you up with the prototype phone?" Linc asked.

Leila lightly touched her swollen cheek. She prodded it for a minute, clearly taking a moment to decide how to answer his question.

"Elijah thought he'd been made and that either Felix or Sam was a plant. He told me a day before we went to that conference room for a meeting. It was supposed to be with the Syrian Minister of Health and Services. Of course, that was going to be all bullshit. Elijah clued me into being the smoother before we left the states. I went to CIA Headquarters and got the phone. They had another phone in the lab that they could do all the bells and whistles. I could grab their data, plant malware, listen in on their conversations, everything."

"Did you meet with Jerry before?" Linc asked.

"He's new to me. I'm pretty sure that if I had met him, I would have skipped the assignment."

Linc looked over at Kostya and saw he was smiling too.

"Well, that explains the phone. When did Elijah tell you about the diamonds?" Linc asked.

"Two or three days ago? Whenever Sunday was. He was worried that either Felix or Sam was a plant. He told me to never be alone with either one of them. How is Sam doing?" she asked.

"He was sitting up when we walked by," Kostya answered. "Do you know about Elijah?"

"His prognosis is good. He's stable. They operated on his brain, and they put him in that coma until his brain stops swelling," Katherine answered.

"That's good to know. Thank you," Kostya smiled at Katherine.

Kostya looked down at his watch. "Linc, we've got to go. Captain Rankin should have transport ready for us to get us into Jordan. We can be airlifted back to the aircraft carrier from there."

"Wait a minute. Katherine, isn't there a pen over there

and some paper?" Leila asked as she pointed to the little table that separated their two beds.

"No, honey, I'm afraid not."

Kostya pulled out a small tablet and a pen. "Here you go."

Leila smiled as she took the pad of paper. She scribbled on it, ripped it off the pad then thrust it at Linc. He took it and looked down. He slowly grinned.

"Call me." She smiled.

"I never saw that," Kostya said as he took back his pen and tablet. "I didn't see a thing."

Linc was still grinning as they loaded into the back of the truck that would haul their asses to Jordan.

11

SHE LOOKED AROUND THE RECEPTION HALL AND REALIZED just how many people had come to Elijah's celebration of life. It made her happy.

"He lived a good life, Honey," her dad said as he put his arm around her shoulders. "He was a widower. Did you know that?" he asked.

Leila shook her head.

"Loved his wife something fierce. After she passed, he put all of his time and attention into his job. He knew he was making a difference in the world."

"I just can't believe that the last time I saw him whole was in Syria." She grabbed a Kleenex out of her purse. "I mean it was bad, but they said he'd eventually be all right."

"Honey, I know him. He would not have wanted to live like that. Nothing they were doing for him here in the States was helping. He wasn't talking, or walking or even understanding anything any of us were saying. He was lost to us before he landed back on US soil."

"I know, but he *was* still alive. I could pretend for a

little longer. I wasn't ready for him to go. Why did he have to throw that clot?"

"It was because of all the trauma, sweetheart," her dad tried to console her.

She looked up into the kind blue eyes of her father and thanked God that he had been promoted up into a desk job in the FBI. Her dad, always knowing what she needed, gave her a hug.

Her little mother came up to the two of them, then placed her hand over Leila's heart. "Come now, *bebek*, we'll go home now. I have baklava waiting for both of you at home. It has raisins, just the way you like it." Leila wrapped her arm around her petite mother and rested her healed cheek against her head.

"Thank you *anne*."

"Leila, you must be really upset to call me *anne*. You haven't called me mom in Turkish in years. It has been so good having you live with us. Have I told you that?"

"Every week since I've moved in."

"I'm going to be sad to see you move back to your townhome next month," her mother pouted as they walked out of the reception hall.

"The sublet lease will be over. I'll have my home back. It's time I moved out of my parent's house," Leila teased.

"You've been such a globetrotter these last few years. We've missed you, Princess," her father said as he ushered them towards his town car. It started to rain as her dad drove the streets of the nation's capital toward their home in Cathedral Heights. The rain matched Leila's mood. The last time she'd really had time with Elijah was when he was being dragged away by Vugar's men. That was a horrible memory. He was so much more than a victim. He was larger than life. As she stared out the car window, she decided to remember the second to last time she saw him. The day before their capture.

He had taken her to a tiny café in Damascus. No one was around, and he laid out everything that was going on. It was the first time he had explained things when she had acted as a translator on one of his little 'missions'. Hell, she'd known this one was going to be more intensive since Langley had sent her out with the space-age-piece-of-shit phone. But she didn't know just how convoluted it was until Elijah laid it out for her.

"You think that Felix or Sam could be a traitor?" she asked in a whisper. She picked up the small cup of strong coffee and took a tiny sip.

Elijah nodded. "Leila, I feel it in my gut that this is a set-up, but we're too far gone to stop now."

"I know this isn't just about some trade agreement with Landry Oil and Katherine's company, Nu-Soyl, but I didn't think you would actually tell me the endgame."

"Leila, I have to. I'm worried that either Sam Phelps or Felix Ratcliff could be a plant. And I'll be damned if I know which one it is, or who their boss is. You're the only one I trust in this fucking mess."

She noted that his hand actually trembled a little bit as he put down the small cup of coffee. She didn't like this. She didn't like this at all.

"Okay, what do you need?"

"There are four prisoners being held by the al-Assad regime. The US has tried all methods to get them released, and nothing has worked. Syria is calling them spies, but they're not. They are just two reporters. One woman was just here to help displaced people, and the fourth is a fucking minister."

"Okay."

Elijah waved for the server to come over, and he lifted his cup. Soon his cup was full again. "The US won't negotiate with terrorists, but a close second is we will not pay a ransom to a foreign country for prisoners. But that's what we're doing. I've got an old friend of mine who works high up in al-Assad's government. He has the juice to release the prisoners."

"Release or help them escape?" Leila asked as she took another small sip of the coffee. You'd think being half Turkish, she'd have a taste for the bitter coffee, but not so much.

"Release. I think my guy is going to give over half the diamonds to al-Assad and keep half for himself."

"What diamonds?"

"The five million dollars' worth of diamonds that a CIA agent assigned to Syria has. All I have to do is call and ask for them."

Leila shook her head. It was a lot of information to take in. She liked Sam Phelps. He seemed like a good guy. Felix was an unknown quantity, but she really didn't want Sam to end up being the fly in the ointment.

"I'm trusting you, Leila. If something goes wrong, I need you to remember these two names, and knowing your memory, that shouldn't be a problem," he laughed. "The man who has the diamonds works at the Jasmine Hotel. His name is Adnan El Din." Leila nodded.

"Repeat it back to me, honey." Leila managed by the skin of her teeth not to roll her eyes. "The CIA agent with the diamonds works at the Jasmine hotel and his name is Adnan El Din. Why does he have them and not you?" she asked.

"That's the agency for you, always trying to make things more convoluted. They just didn't want one person with all the information to also have all the assets. All I have to do is contact him, and he'll produce them."

"Okay, give me the next one."

"This man is trickier. A lot of time he works out of al-Assad's palace, here in Damascus. He's very influential. He and I have known each other longer than you've been alive. Nobody knows who he is but me. And now you. His name is Shaker Jassim. The way to get ahold of him is encrypted email. You provide my name, a number, and times you can be reached, and he'll call you."

"He can really get the prisoners released?"

"Absolutely. He's turned into quite an information broker here in Syria. If al-Assad ever found out about it, he and his family would be dead. Right now, Shaker is trying to build a big enough nest egg so he can get him and his extended family to America."

"Okay, give me the email address." Elijah spit it out and Leila memorized it.

"But you don't think something will actually happen, do you?"

"I'm ninety percent sure that nothing will happen, but I've got an itch on the back of my neck. When that happens, I build contingency plans, on top of contingency plans."

The car stopped moving and Leila realized she was actually in Washington DC and her father had just pulled up to her childhood home.

"You okay, Leila?" her mother asked as she looked into the backseat. "I know you loved Elijah."

"I'm okay, Mom. I'm just thankful to be home."

Linc strolled up to his lieutenant's office. He would have gone in, but it was pretty crowded. Lark was inside, in all her pregnant glory. She looked to be about six months pregnant and Linc had never seen Kostya smile so big.

Gideon was standing right outside the door. "Do you need something?" he asked.

That was Gideon. He was always in tune to the men of Omega Sky.

"I was stopping by to see if I could get some leave."

Gideon gave him a slow grin. "Does this have anything to do with the fact that you're so pretty?"

Dammit. I knew I'd be hearing about this forever.

"It might," he confessed.

"Have you gotten a hold of her?"

"She and I have traded voicemails and emails. She said she'd make herself available whenever I could make it up to DC, or she'd come down to Virginia Beach."

Gideon's expression changed. "She's willing to come here for a date? That's cool."

Linc grinned. "That's what I thought too. But it's not how I want things to start. I'm going to go rent a room at a nice hotel, and we'll see the sights, have dinner, maybe dance. The whole nine yards."

"That sounds like a good plan."

"Wanted to get Thursday to Monday off."

"Put it into the system. I'll let Kostya know I approved it."

"Thanks," Linc said with a grin.

"Since it's slow today, why don't you leave early and get an early start on your trip?" Gideon suggested.

Linc's smile went brighter. "I'll do that."

Linc left the Little Creek base with a spring in his step. He headed to his town home and got packed. His good suit was still in the dry-cleaning wrapper from the last time he'd worn it, so that was taken care of. He sat down at his laptop and checked out hotels in the DC area and flinched when he saw the prices.

When he saw the pictures of the rooms, he was even more surprised.

Four hundred a night for this?

Too bad it was DC instead of New York, because then he'd text Jada, Gideon's fiancé. She knew her way around the city.

"Amy!" he called out.

Amy Linden, Ryker's woman, fiancée, whatever, would know all about DC He pulled out his phone and texted her for some recommendations.

He waited, then his phone rang.

Shit. Now I'm going to have to answer questions.

"Hi Amy," he answered the phone.

"Hi Prettyboy," she laughed.

Linc groaned. "Everybody knows what she said, right?"

"Oh yeah. I think that kind of gossip made its way to the West Coast."

Linc looked heavenward but knew he would not get any help from there.

"Can you help me feel not so bad about that?" Linc asked.

"Sure. What's up?"

"I'm going up to DC for a couple of days. I'm renting a room, and I'd like to come home and not have to eat only peanut butter and jelly sandwiches for the next month."

Amy giggled. "That's DC for you. Those rates are killer. And that's before you see what the parking costs."

"You mean parking isn't included with that highway robbery?"

"Fraid not."

"Is there any hotel you can recommend that is nice, but a little more reasonable?" Linc asked hopefully.

"Why do you need it? That will help me know what to look for."

"I'm going up there to meet a woman. We really haven't had much time together, so I'd like to make a good first impression."

"Does she live in DC?"

"Yes."

"Okay, let me make a few phone calls. I'll call you back."

"Thanks."

Linc finished packing, then called Jase. "Where'd you go? I was looking for you. Gideon wants to hand us our asses next week on some night combat swimming training. He's found someplace new to take us. You're an asshole sometimes, but I wanted to make sure you were on my team."

Linc laughed. Jase was his best friend on the team. Calling him an asshole was his version of being nice.

"Gideon let me out early to play. I'm going up to DC to spend time with Leila."

"You mean the woman that you haven't spoken to since you've returned to the states? The woman that you haven't seen for three months? That woman?"

"Remember, we were in Venezuela for six weeks after Syria. There hasn't been a lot of time for us to connect. It's not like she's been blowing me off."

There was a pause. Linc braced. "Just remember, you two were together during stressful conditions. Don't expect that same level of attraction to necessarily be there when you meet up again," Jase cautioned.

Linc had heard it all before.

"Jase. Do I need to explain it to you again? It wasn't just Syria. We were into one another in Turkey too. We both tried to look one another up. Now, I'm not looking for the love of my life, but I am looking to find out what this could be. She's the most interesting woman I've ever met, and I'm not going to let her slip through my fingers."

"Well, there's also the fact she's agreed to go out with you. That doesn't happen all that much for you, so you gotta make hay while the sun shines."

"You do know you're an asshole, don't you?" Linc asked his friend.

"It's one of my best traits."

Linc laughed, then his phone beeped. "Gotta go, Ryker's Amy is calling me back. Hopefully, she has a line on a place in DC that won't rob me blind."

Jase laughed. "If she tells you about one, share."

"Will do."

Linc switched over to Amy.

"Hi."

"Hi Linc. How invested are you in DC?"

"What do you mean?"

"You told me she lives in DC, so I figured she might like a change of pace. Who really wants to stay in a hotel in the city they live in, you know?"

"I'm listening."

"A good friend of mine's dad owns a boutique hotel in the Shenandoah National Park. I've been planning on dragging Ryker there, so if you take me up on this, don't tell him about it, okay?"

"Mum's the word."

"Anyway, I already checked. Somebody just canceled their reservation, so he's got a two-room suite available for a long weekend. Normally these go for over a grand a night. Instead, this will cost you three hundred a night. Trust me, take it."

Linc grinned. This was perfect!

"Amy, you're a goddess! I will definitely take it. Thank you so much. Who do I need to call to reserve it?"

Amy gave him all the details.

Linc hung up and went to his computer. He immediately booked the hotel, then texted Leila to find out if he could pick her up early.

He got an immediate response back.

> Leila: You don't have to pick me up, I can always meet you someplace, but early would be wonderful.

> Linc: How do you feel about a getaway in the Shenandoah Valley?

Linc cringed when the bubbles kept popping up, showing that Leila was writing a long text.

God, he sounded like he wanted to sleep with her right off the bat. Before she could finish, he typed again.

> Linc: A friend hooked me up with a two-bedroom suite.

> Leila: I've only been there one time, but it was beautiful. A lot of the clothes that I have with me are for winter, so that would be perfect. When are you thinking you could pick me up?

Linc did some quick math. It would take him six hours to get to DC, and then two hours to get to the hotel. If he left now, they should be able to get to the hotel at dusk. And there really had been no snow since late January, so the roads should be good.

> Linc: I should hit your place about fifteen hundred hours. How does that sound?

> Leila: Fifteen hundred hours, sounds all sexy Navy speak. That's how it sounds.

Linc chuckled.

> Linc: I look forward to meeting your parents.

> Leila: My dad looks forward to meeting you.

This time Linc winced. Her dad was pretty high up in the FBI. He'd had Gideon do a little digging. He'd bet the farm that her dad had done a little digging as well.

> Linc: Okay, see you then.

12

LEILA OPENED THE DOOR TWO SECONDS AFTER HE KNOCKED.

Sure, I wasn't excited at all about seeing him again.

"Hi." She grinned.

Oh, those eyes. Those beautiful blue eyes.

"Hello, Leila."

She stared.

Had she called him pretty? He was gorgeous.

"It's so good to see you. Especially under happier circumstances. And when I don't have two black eyes."

"You looked fantastic then, and you look fantastic now. Here." He handed her a bouquet of flowers. "These are for your mother."

Leila took them. She sniffed the white rose and poinsettia arrangement. "She'll love it."

"She'll love it even more if you invited the boy inside out of the cold."

Leila looked over her shoulder at her mother and blushed. She turned back to Linc. "Dammit, where are my manners? Come on inside. We have coffee, tea, or hot chocolate for you."

Linc chuckled as he stepped inside.

"Hello, Lincoln, my name is Miray Cloud. Please come in and sit. My husband is on a phone call, but he'll be with us shortly."

"Here, Mom," Leila said as she thrust the bouquet at her mother. "These are for you. Linc brought them."

Her mother laughed. "Yes, I know, *Bebek*."

Leila peeked over at Linc. She would have felt embarrassed except he had a huge grin on his face too, so she knew he was just as excited to see her.

But gah!

Could she sound any more like a sixteen-year-old going to a prom?

"*Bebek*, let's get your young man in out of the cold."

"Come on in, Linc. We're in the kitchen."

"That's where my family usually huddles." He smiled. "Mom, my little brothers and sisters, and my dad are always in the kitchen eating whatever she's cooking, even now that we're adults. And don't worry about the cold. I'm from Minnesota, so this is nothing."

Mrs. Cloud led the way to the kitchen and Leila watched Linc's face as he studied the windows overlooking their big backyard. Even in February, her mother managed to make the entire area look nice, with fairy lights in the trees and potted plants.

"This is a great space," Linc said.

"My mom does it."

"Miray has a green thumb, that's for sure."

Leila and Linc turned around as her father walked in from the other side of the kitchen. He was only one or two inches shorter than Linc, but he had the same kind of presence.

"Dad, I'd like you to meet Lincoln Hart. He's one of the

men who rescued me in Syria. I know I'm not supposed to talk about it, but I am to you and Mom. He saved my life."

She watched as Linc blushed.

Too cute for words.

"You will have my undying gratitude," her dad said as he walked up and held out his hand to Linc. "I'm Grant Cloud. I'm sure Leila's told you. I work for the FBI."

"Sit. Everyone sit. I have the drinks ready. What would you like?" Miray asked.

"Coffee would be great," Linc said.

"How do you like it?"

"Black."

"It's very strong," Leila warned.

"Even better," Linc said as he stood standing until both Miray and Leila were seated. Leila could see her dad's smile of approval.

"Aren't the flowers nice? Linc brought them for Mom."

"They're very nice." Her father smiled. "So Linc, it's a little odd for you to be dating my daughter since you met her on one of your missions, isn't it?"

Shit.

Linc looked her father straight in the eye. "It is. I don't know if Leila had a chance to tell you, but we first met in Turkey when she was working as a translator for another operation. She was acting as a co-worker, not a hostage. I was lucky enough to find out that we were both trying to get in touch with one another after that operation, but we failed to find one another."

"Mmmh," Grant said as he took a sip of his coffee. He reached for the creamer, the same as she did.

"This is excellent coffee," Linc said to her mom. "I got a taste for it when I was working overseas."

Her mom grinned. "I have some baklava to go with it."

Linc looked at his watch. "I think we need to skip it. I really don't want to be driving your daughter on unfamiliar roads after dark, if I can help it."

Leila peeked up at her father under her lashes.

Cha-ching!

Linc couldn't have said anything better than to say he wanted to take good care of Grant Cloud's baby girl.

LINC STOWED Leila's backpack and small suitcase into the back of his truck, then helped her climb up. She hadn't worn high heels; instead her boots were flat. *Smart woman*.

"Since you're the passenger, you get to choose the music."

"I think you've got that wrong. He who drives gets to choose the music, but I'll go with it. Give me your phone. I'll pick something of yours. It'll be fun to see what your taste in music is."

Leila went through his phone, selected something, and soon he heard *Thunder* by Imagine Dragons playing. At a red light, he quickly glanced over at her. He could tell by her smile that she was really enjoying the music and hadn't picked it out thinking it was something he might like.

Sweet.

It wasn't until they were out of DC proper and on I-66 that he was ready to talk. Before he had a chance to say anything, Leila turned down the volume.

"So. Lincoln Hart. Tell me a bit about yourself. I mean, besides being some kind of superhero and all, who are you?"

"I'm thinking that's like the pot calling the kettle black. How is it a geology graduate student in Turkey, who works part time as a translator, finds herself in such capricious situations?"

"Hmmmm, capricious. Good word."

"I've been reading the dictionary in my spare time so I could sound educated enough to keep up with you."

Leila laughed. It sounded almost like music. It actually flowed over him, smooth like caramel syrup.

"How much digging did your comp guy do on me?" Leila asked.

"A little. How much digging did your dad do on me?"

"A little."

Now it was his turn to laugh. "But seriously. I know that the geology part that I heard in Turkey was bullshit, and you'd already completed your Masters in Global Affairs. I know you spent a year in the CIA."

"I know you joined the Navy when you were eighteen. I know you went into SEAL training late, not until you were twenty-one. And I know you were second in your class in Navy SEAL sniper school. Some guy named Finn Crandall came in first."

"Your dad sure does dig deep."

"He doesn't know a lot of personal stuff. I know your team members' names. Stuff like that. But I want to know about you."

"Same goes. I figure that's what this weekend is all about."

"I'm hoping for some hiking. These are just my all-around boots. I also packed thick socks and sturdy hiking boots."

Linc smiled. It just kept getting better and better.

They started talking about one another's work.

Nothing deep, just funny stories about people. He knew that she probably signed NDAs for a lot of her assignments and she was smart enough to know that he couldn't really talk about any of the stuff that he did.

"...so there I was, holding a baby, with a toddler tugging on my skirt and the Russian Under Secretary was continuing to ask me questions about the upcoming conference. I'm like hello, don't you see that your wife just dropped your kids, literally, in my lap? And why the hell didn't she drop them in *your* lap?"

"You're kidding me, right?"

"Nope, I'm not. So here he is, too good to deal with his own kids, but I'm supposed to be a nanny and his translator at the same time."

"What did you do?"

"This was early in my career. I was only twenty-three, so I put up with it. But, when he asks me if, and I quote, if I would consider being his mistress for the summer, then I lost it."

"Tell me there was someone, an American, that you could report him to."

"Nope, he was my boss. I'd hired on for a five-month gig. I handed him his baby and walked out. Luckily, I wasn't living on the premises. I immediately went to the American consulate and told them what had happened. There wasn't much they could do except expedite my flight home and work with my landlord to get me out of my lease early."

"Jesus, I just can't imagine that happening. I guess it's different in Russia."

"There's still a lot of chauvinism here in the US. I talk to my friends about it. Because the job I have is more white-collar, I don't get it quite as much, but some of my other friends bump into it a lot."

"Hmmm. I don't have stories like that, I just have stories of my friends being dumbasses. Well, actually, I like that Lark, Kostya's wife, led him a merry chase before they truly got together."

"A merry chase, huh?"

"Yeah. You might have heard of her. Her name is Lark Sorensen. She's a reporter."

"I think I have. She does in-depth pieces? Something about those slums in Brazil, right?"

"Yep, that's her. I can't tell you how she and Kostya met."

"Ah-ha!"

"What, ah-ha?" Linc knew what she was talking about. His Leila wasn't a dumb girl.

"She's like us. Kostya met her on a mission. Didn't he?"

Linc cleared his throat. "As I was saying, when Lark and Kostya met at a bar in DC, she ended up having some troubles with one of her current stories."

"What kind of troubles?"

"Suffice it to say that some of her leads were pretty unsavory and Kostya watched her six. It was great because Lark's best friend is now Ryker's girlfriend."

"When did all this happen?"

"A couple of years ago. At least the part with Lark and Kostya. Ryker and Amy were still dating when we were in Turkey," Linc answered.

"Sounds like some of my friends. It's the age. People are pairing up. I don't know if it's a good thing or a bad thing."

"Oh, I'm thinking it's a good thing." Linc reached out

and picked up Leila's hand and twined his fingers with hers, then brought it to rest on his thigh. "It has to be the right person, and if it is, then pairing up is definitely a good thing."

13

"This place is beautiful, Linc. I don't think I've ever stayed in any place so luxurious unless I was working with some high-falutin' ambassador overseas. Are your parents millionaires and I don't know it?"

Linc laughed out loud. "Hardly. I'm just as blown away as you are."

He dropped the bags in the middle of the living room. There was a fireplace in front of a sofa and two winged-back chairs. They were definitely going to be making use of that sofa. He strolled over to the coffee table and saw that there was a bottle chilling in a silver bucket and two empty flutes. He picked up the card and saw that the bottle of champagne was a welcome from Amy's friend's dad. The card also said the meals were included with their stay.

What the hell?

He'd have to get the scoop from Amy when he got home.

"Champagne?" Leila asked.

"Yeah. This is a lot more than I ever expected."

"It's good to have friends," Leila smiled. "Do you care which room is yours? They both have bathrooms attached."

"Nope, you choose. I'm going to get a fire started."

"That sounds good."

It didn't take him long to have the fire going. He picked up the room service menu and saw that there was more to choose from than he would have expected from such a small hotel.

"That feels nice," Leila said as she came out of her room. "Is that the room service menu?" She asked as she looked over his shoulder.

"Yep. Most of the meals are for two people to share."

"Imagine that. You're not a vegetarian, are you?" Leila asked as he handed her the menu.

"Not hardly."

"Good. Because the chateaubriand looks yummy, especially with the mashed potatoes."

"I'm liking this get-to-know-you part of the relationship already. That was what I was thinking, too."

"A good midwestern boy who likes meat and potatoes, go figure."

She brushed up against him as she put down the menu, then turned back to look at him, ensuring that they were touching, breast to chest.

"Relationship, huh?" she asked.

"Relationship?"

"You said get-to-know-you part of the relationship. Are we in a relationship, Mr. Hart?"

Linc swallowed. Then went for it. "For somebody I've only seen face to face maybe five times, I gotta say I'm more emotionally invested in you than I have been with any other woman in my life."

Leila's beautiful brown eyes widened, and he watched them turn almost black. She brought her hands up and let them rest on his chest. He felt her touch, like an electrical current, throughout his body. "You really lay it on the line, don't you?" she asked.

"I learned early in life that life's too short. Don't put up with the bad, and when you find the good, hang on with your very life. It might be too early, but I'm thinking you're my good."

He dropped his hands so that they rested on her hips.

"Kiss me, Linc."

He wrapped one of his arms around her lower back, then stroked the other one up her spine to her neck. He tangled his fingers through her silky hair and touched his lips to hers. Once. Twice. She sighed. Then he plundered.

She tasted a little bit like coffee, but mostly like Leila. He needed more. Her hand came up and cupped his cheek. It was a lovely feeling that made him feel cared for. Then her hand moved and pressed against the back of his neck. She needed more, too.

Leila bit his lower lip and he couldn't help but laugh.

"You're a hellion, aren't you?"

"I've been dreaming of your bottom lip for months. Here, let me make it feel better," she offered. Leila opened her mouth, then slowly licked his lip with her glistening tongue. Linc thought his knees would give way.

He pressed a kiss to the side of her lips, then followed a path to right behind her earlobe. He tugged at her lobe with his teeth while licking the little morsel with his tongue.

"Ahhhhh," Leila moaned. "Again."

Linc smiled to himself as he bit her earlobe again. He gave her hair one gentle tug so that her head and neck were exposed. He scattered kisses down her jaw, gently on the cheek that had been broken, then rained kisses and licks along her neck until he reached the boat collar of her cream-colored sweater.

She pressed her pelvis closer to his and did a little shimmy.

So sexy.

A phone rang.

Dammit.

"Dammit," Leila sighed. "Please say that isn't mine, because I specifically turned mine off."

Linc looked down at the end table where the room service table was. "No, it's the hotel phone. I'll answer it, and we might as well order our food, too. See what you want to drink, and what you would like for dessert."

"Hello?" Linc answered.

"Mr. Hart. I'm just calling to see if everything is to your liking. Is there anything that we might provide for you?"

Fancy.

"No, we're covered. We were just going to call down to the restaurant for dinner. We wanted room service."

"Let me connect you."

There was a pause.

"Chocolate lava cake?" Leila asked hopefully. "Plus a side of vanilla ice cream?"

"Definitely. How do you want the meat cooked?"

"I usually like mine medium rare, but I'm open."

Linc smiled. "A girl after my own heart."

When he was connected, Linc put in the order. By the time he was done, Leila had found the sound system in the room and had connected her phone to it. This time the singer was someone that Linc didn't recognize, but he liked him.

Leila was standing near the bay windows that looked over the woods they would hopefully hike through tomorrow. He went and stood next to her. She held out her hand and he gripped it. They stood there for a long moment.

"You know, I wasn't kidding about you being a superhero. I was sure we were going to die."

Linc thought about how he'd found her in that hole. There she was, shivering, her hair matted, two black eyes where she'd been obviously beaten, sitting on her knees in filthy water, holding up Katherine on her lap as she hummed *YMCA*.

"You weren't going to die, Leila. I've never met someone who is more of a fighter than you are. I'm betting if you met the devil at the gates of hell, you'd laugh in his face."

Leila turned and looked at him. "Then you're seeing someone who isn't me. I quit the CIA because I was scared."

"But when the chips were down in Syria, you did what you had to do. That's my definition of bravery."

He could see her assessing him. "If you're looking for someone like a special operations person to be in a relationship with, I'm not your girl. I'm average, and that's all I want to be. Average. Dad's the one in the FBI. I only did things with Elijah because he promised it would be translator work that wouldn't be quite as boring as the political stuff I normally do. I trusted Elijah, that he would keep me safe. Did you know he was my godfather?"

Linc shook his head, waiting for her to say more.

"That time in Turkey was an anomaly too."

"Are you done?" he asked.

She nodded.

"Leila, I get all the adrenaline I need from my job. I'll admit that a lot of guys that I work with, at least the younger ones, are adrenaline junkies. They need their fixes even during their leaves. They'll go mountain climbing in the Andes, or scuba dive uncharted waters, or they'll go ATV off-roading in Alaska. I'm not them."

"You're not?"

"Nope. I love my job. I'm good at my job. I love serving my country. But when I have downtime, I'm down. My idea of a good time might be sailing, reading a good book, going back home and spending time with my family. Hell, I haven't mentioned this to the team, but I've taken time off to go babysit my sister's kids. So, average and normal sounds good to me."

He watched as her shoulders seemed to relax.

"That's good to know."

There was a knock on the door.

"I'll get it. I don't know about you, but I'm pretty hungry," Linc said.

"Me too."

LEILA WISHED that she'd slept better so that she would be in a little better shape for this hike. Unfortunately, all she could think about was the make-out session with Linc on the couch, and how bummed she was that it didn't turn into anything more.

"There's nothing that says we have to do the whole hike to the ridge," Linc said as they took another break. "I'm just enjoying hiking in this part of the country at a leisurely pace. Normally any hiking I'm doing, I have a seventy-pound backpack on my back, and I have to move my ass to keep up with the others. This is wonderful."

"You're so full of shit. I'm holding you back." Leila took another sip from her water bottle.

Linc took a step closer to her. "You sure are skilful when it comes to saying what I would expect from you. Is there a reason?"

Leila put her water bottle back in her pack and thought.

"I'm not really sure, but you're right. I do keep doing that, don't I?"

"You sure do. I only know English, Spanish, and a smattering of Arabic. Would you expect me to keep up with you in a foreign country where you knew the language? Would you get frustrated with me?"

"Of course not."

They fell into a gentler pace, and Leila was happy about that.

"Your dad doesn't seem like the type of guy who would put unreasonable expectations on you, but I could have read him wrong. I only spent twenty minutes with the guy."

"No, it's not Dad. It's not Mom either."

As they picked their way through the winter woods, Leila thought about her time spent in Turkey with her grandparents, aunts, uncles, and cousins, and she laughed.

"What?" Linc asked gently.

"I figured it out. I spent every other summer in Turkey with my grandparents. It was great. I got to find out about different cultures, and it expanded my horizons. I love my *nene* and *dede* but a lot of times my cousins would come over. They were older than me, and when I think about it, they rode me hard. Not that they expected it of me, it was to put me down. Put me in my place and prove that they were better than their rich American cousin."

"Doesn't sound like a lot of fun," Linc said as he helped her over a log.

"Don't get me wrong. I love my family in Turkey, and they sure as hell don't do that kind of thing anymore. That was just kid stuff. But you're right, it sticks with me today. Especially about physical things. We were always playing soccer, and I couldn't seem to stop the ball or to hold on to it to save my life. We also played basketball, and they thought because I was tall, I'd be good at that, but I washed out. Just couldn't do it."

"So, your need to meet or exceed really comes out in physical activities," Linc said thoughtfully.

"Yeah, and with you being a frickin' SEAL, I kind of will never measure up."

"I gotta say, Leila, I have never been attracted to one of my teammates. Even though they can all keep up."

She laughed as Linc pulled back another branch. Suddenly, Leila saw they were standing on the ridge that had been described in the brochure.

"This is breathtaking."

"Breathtaking," Linc agreed.

She turned to look at him and saw that he was looking at her.

"You are, you know. You're the most beautiful woman I have ever seen."

The way he said it, with all the emotion behind his words, made her feel like it. She stepped up to him and twined her arms around his neck. "How about we practice kissing outside?"

"I think that is a marvellous idea."

14

"I NEED A SHOWER," WERE THE FIRST WORDS OUT OF LEILA'S mouth when they got back to the room.

"Really? I would have thought you would go for a bath after a six-mile hike."

Leila looked over at him. "You actually kind of read my mind. It just seemed rude."

"It's not rude at all. We've both been hopping with our jobs. This is definitely our time to get to know one another, but this is also our vacation time."

"Okay, you talked me into it. A bath. But instead of room service tonight, how about we go out to dinner? I actually did a little sleuthing. I was going to bring something dressy to go out, but this really isn't the place for it. But I can always dress up for you sometime in DC. Instead, I thought we could go to the Skyline restaurant. It has nothing as fancy as the Chateaubriand, but it does have...wait for it...homemade blackberry ice cream."

"I'm sold."

Hell, to see her this excited, he'd have sour lemon ice cream.

"Go take your bath. I'm going to take a shower and watch some TV. And Leila, for God's sake, take your time. There's no rush."

"Thanks, Linc."

Linc went into his bedroom and got out of his hiking clothes. He'd packed enough so he wouldn't have to wear anything twice. After all, he was out to make a good impression. Leila was something else. She had really calmed down on the hike back to the hotel. Once she realized she didn't have to race him, they had a great time. He kind of wanted to go back in time and throttle those cousins of hers. But, the way they had made her think just might have had a hand in creating the woman who did so well during that god-awful situation in Syria.

He tried to concentrate on what all Leila had been through as he got into the shower instead of what it felt like to kiss her and how good her ass looked in her jeans when they were hiking. He'd been hoping for another room service dinner that might wind up turning into something a lot more satisfying than just making out on the sofa.

He looked down at his hopeful penis as he walked into the luxurious shower.

"Down, boy. We haven't gotten our go orders yet."

He started lathering up, but he noticed that his cock still hadn't got the message that he didn't get to come out and play until blackberry ice cream was eaten.

God, the way it felt when she'd bit his bottom lip, then licked away the hurt with her glistening tongue, had crept into his dreams all night long.

Fuck it. There was no way he could squire Ms. Cloud around with a rampant hard-on. He needed to do something about it. He took his dick in hand and while thinking of Leila, he broke a record in getting relief.

"Now, that's all you're getting until she says otherwise. You got that?"

He knew that reprimanding his dick was hopeless. He hadn't been this horny and hopeful since he was fifteen.

DURING HER BATH, Leila had decided that there was something a lot more satisfying than blackberry ice cream —it didn't matter if it was homemade. She hadn't been sure she was going to wear the sexy lingerie, during this trip or not. She had prayed she and Linc would have chemistry, but there had always been the off chance that they'd leave each other flat.

Leila grinned as she pulled on her thong panties, then she took her time rolling on her sheer black stockings with the seam in the back. She loved this lingerie set. One of the best things about her time in France had been the shopping, especially the lingerie shopping.

She clipped the stockings to the garter, then wiggled herself into the bustier. Instead of red trim, there was seafoam green. It was kick-ass. She put on the barely there seafoam lace and silk robe and she was set.

Leila heard the television on out in the living room. It'd been on for a while. But then again, she'd taken a long while to get ready. She brushed out her wet hair, then blew it dry with the diffuser. It was shiny and manageable, just the way she liked it. She knew Linc liked it that way too, since he sure as hell played with it a lot while they'd made out on the couch.

She usually wasn't this nervous about having sex. But Lincoln Hart was special. She'd thought that when she first met him over a year ago in Turkey but then...when he saved her in Syria...well.

She opened her bedroom door and walked out. She'd only taken two steps towards the couch before he'd already sat up and turned to look at her. He stumbled as he got to his feet.

"Let me turn this off," he muttered.

She grinned as she watched him search unsuccessfully for the remote. He finally found it and turned off the TV.

"I've decided to pass on the blackberry ice cream tonight," Leila told him.

Is that my voice? Why does it sound so breathy?

He prowled over to her and she got the fun of watching how his Henley shirt molded to all of those big, beautiful shoulder muscles. He was so sexy. She looked up. His smile was predatory.

"To hell with ice cream. I'm seeing the dessert I really want right in front of me," Linc said as he stopped a foot away. "Does this mean what I think it means?" he asked as he traced his finger down from her shoulder to the tip of her finger.

She shivered.

"If you think it means I want to fuck you, then you're right."

Linc threw back his head and laughed. "My God, woman, you just keep getting better and better. I'll have you know that being a good boy scout, I actually brought condoms with me in case fucking ever became part of this weekend's agenda," he grinned down at her.

Leila relaxed. She wasn't quite at the point where she

wanted to get all mushy and call it making love, nor did she want to just say have sex...but fuck? Oh yeah. She was all over that.

Linc brushed back her hair and kissed the tendon on her neck. "If your condoms are within easy reach, maybe your room?" she suggested.

"How about moving over to the fire for a few minutes? I want to see you in the firelight. All your body's curves, dips, and treasures."

"Th-that sounds good," she stuttered.

"Your robe is all kinds of beautiful, but how about we get this off you, so I can have you walk in front of me as we go to the fire? Would you do that for me, beautiful?"

Before she could even say yes, Linc was slipping the lace and silk off her shoulders and it puddled to the floor. "Just saying, that was awful pretty, but what was underneath is far prettier."

Linc traced the top of her bustier with both fingers until they met in the middle. "I like how you wrap presents." His voice was lower. It sounded like his tongue had just a bit of roughened velvet on it, and his words had to pass over it before coming out to flow over her.

Won't a rough, velvet tongue feel good on other things?

She stared up at him, her lips parted, begging for a kiss.

"No kisses yet. I want to see your sexy ass swaying as you walk over to the fireplace. You had me hard almost the entire hike. This is my prize for being a gentleman and not pushing you up against a tree and having my way with you."

Leila laughed. She walked past him and made sure to put a little more swing in her step as she walked.

"You're killing me, Leila. Your stockings have seams, and you're wearing a garter belt."

"Really? I didn't notice."

She watched as he closed the curtains in the living room. Their room looked over the forest. Even so, at night with their room lit up it would be easy for someone to peek in. Her heart melted. That was just who Lincoln Hart was, he was a caretaker.

Again, he prowled across the room to stand in front of her, and then, ever so slowly, he knelt. Leila shivered. He went to work on her garters.

"Do you know how sensuous a woman is when she wears stockings and garters?" Linc asked.

She could only shake her head.

He unsnapped one, then two, then three, then the final one.

"Let me tell you what it does to a man when a woman wears such enticing underwear. It acts like one of the strongest aphrodisiacs in the world. The lacier it is, the more we want to tear it off the woman's body and find out what's underneath. It's like at Christmas, you always want to open the prettiest package."

Before Linc rolled down her stocking, he nudged her just a little, and she widened her stance. Then he kissed her on the top of her thigh, above her stocking and below her panties. Leila's legs trembled.

"Oh no, you're a strong woman. You can take it. No falling down on the job now," Linc teased. He rolled the first stocking off her leg, then when it got to her foot, she put one hand on his shoulder and he took it entirely off.

Again, as he unsnapped her garter and rolled off her other stocking he spoke to her. Mesmerizing her with words like *ravishing* and *tantalizing*. Now she had both hands on his shoulders to keep upright.

Linc stood up and took a step back. "I was right. You do look luscious in the firelight. But I want to see more."

15

THANK GOD LEILA'S TREMBLING, OTHERWISE SHE'D CATCH onto the fact that I can barely keep my hands steady enough to work the hooks on her damned bustier!

"Fuck, baby, your tits are gorgeous."

Leila giggled. "A dirty talker. Could this get any better?"

"That's my line." Linc stopped trying to unfasten the corset and instead traced the back of his fingers down the gentle slopes of her breasts. He was glad to see her nipples were diamond-hard. He so wanted her on the same page that he was on.

"I love your skin. It's so soft and delicate, it makes me want to lick you up." He swept her up into his arms and placed her gently onto the plush rug in front of the fireplace. He looked down on her face, and he could see she was as swept away as he was. Then she lifted her right hand and her thumb traced over his lower lip.

"If you love my skin, then I love your mouth. Especially this lip. It's pouty and perfect for kissing."

"Is that a request, Ms. Cloud?"

"I'm sorry. Was that not clear enough for you, Mr. Hart?"

Linc leaned forward and licked his tongue along the seam of her lips, reveling as she whined. He did it again, and she whined again. Then she nipped at his bottom lip and he laughed. He wrapped his arms around her waist and brought her up to him and thrust his tongue into her mouth. One of them was gasping, the other groaning. He was pulling her hair; she was scraping his scalp with her nails. It hurt good. Again and again, their tongues dueled as he fought to get to the essence of Leila Cloud. She broke away.

"Off."

"Hmm?"

"I want your shirt off. Need your naked chest. I've dreamed of your naked chest. I want to make sure that I got it right when I was taking care of myself."

His eyes lit up as he placed her back on the rug, then yanked his shirt over his head. Before he had a chance to say a word, both of her hands were splayed wide on his chest.

"So good. So hard. It's even better than I pictured."

Linc grabbed her wrists. "Wait just a minute, Leila. I want to hear more about you taking care of yourself. That sounds mighty interesting to me. I'm thinking that this could require some study."

"Shut up and let me play," she said as she wrenched her hands loose and started stroking his chest. Linc closed his eyes and let fire streak through his bloodstream as she stroked him. Then, when she sat up and took one of his nipples into her mouth, he shouted.

"Damn!"

It didn't slow her one bit. She wrapped her other arm around his waist, trying to get him closer. He had to get things back in hand. He had a little spitfire in the room with him, and wasn't he a lucky man?

"Oh, no you don't," he said as he pulled himself away from her. "I'm not done unwrapping my present."

Leila pushed out her bottom lip.

"Are you trying to pout to get your way?" he asked.

"It depends."

"On what?"

"Will I get my way?" Leila asked.

Linc shouted with laughter. "Nope, not this time, at least. I have a mission, and you know how strongly I take my missions. Right now, my mission is to see Leila naked in the firelight."

Her eyes closed and her expression turned dreamy as she smiled. "What happens after that?"

"Well, like with any new toy, I get to play with it."

Her eyes snapped open. "Oh, no you don't. You only talked about looking, Buster. Any playing that goes on is going to be a two-way-street, close to some condoms in your bedroom."

"We'll see."

Linc bent down and sucked her lower lip into his mouth, and laved it with his tongue. At the same time, he cupped both of her breasts in his hands and rolled her nipples with his fingers. She arched high against him. "God, yes." She exclaimed.

"Like that, huh?"

"Yes," she sighed.

He went in for another kiss and cupped and molded her firm breasts that felt like silk in his rough hands. When he brushed her tips with his thumb, she wrenched her head away from his kiss. "Harder," she demanded.

He gave the lady what she wanted.

After long minutes, he stopped his ministrations and started to undo the last hooks on her bustier. He helped her lift out of it.

"Dips and curves. I knew it."

He stroked from under her arm, along her side to her waist, then around her hip down to her thigh. "You are perfect."

"Hardly," she snorted.

"You're perfect for me." Before she could say anything more, he wanted the rest of his treat. Linc tucked his fingers into the bows at each side of her sheer panties and tugged them down her long legs. When she was finally naked, he looked into her eyes.

"Sailor, you—"

Before she could start again with her smart mouth, he pressed his body over hers, and caught her mouth in a dazzling kiss. He brought her arms up over her head and prodded her legs apart so that he could lie between them.

Again, he heard her sigh. She undulated, scraping her breasts against the hair on his chest. He felt her press harder. His woman liked a firmer touch, and he was happy to oblige. Linc wasn't aware how long they lay there kissing, learning one another's bodies. Finally, he let go and she got her hands between them and pressed against his chest.

"Can we make love now?" she whispered. "You know. Go to your room and stuff?"

Linc smiled. She was right about that; it would be making love. But she was wrong about where. They weren't quite ready to go to his room. He'd had quite the shower fantasy, and he wasn't about to give it up.

LEILA FELT like she was floating. Was he carrying her? Was she on drugs?

Oh, no. Good kisses. Lots and lots and lots of wonderful kisses.

She opened her eyes and saw almost white-blue eyes. Arctic-blue eyes, but they were so warm.

She shook her head. She needed to get a grip.

"What are you doing?"

"Just looking."

He was stroking, too. Leila turned her head to look at the fire, but it wasn't where she thought it would be. Now her head was pointed toward the sofa and her legs were pointed at the fire.

Wait a minute.

He was kneeling between her legs, and he was still in his jeans.

He pushed her right knee up and out, then looked down and smiled. "I was so right. Seeing you glisten underneath the firelight is the sexiest thing I have ever seen."

Leila wanted to be embarrassed.

I should be embarrassed, right?

Linc brought his hand down and covered her, then he brushed his fingers through the lips of her pussy and electricity arced through her from her toes to the tips of her hair. He did it again, and again.

"Look at you. You're so wet for me, Leila. You have

such a pretty pussy. You know I'm going to have to lick it. Savor it. Suck on your clit. You know that, don't you?"

Leila whined. She needed to rub her legs together to ease the ache.

When she tried, Linc's hands were there to stop her. He scooched down until one arm rested across her stomach while the other hand remained where it had been, touching her in a place that was making her go insane.

The first swipe of his tongue shocked her. She needed a moment to get used to it, to catch her breath, but did he allow that? No. The second swipe of his tongue went deeper. She felt his tongue curl.

"You taste so good," he said in that low, sexy voice.

The next swipe of his tongue included a finger entering her body. Slowly. Gently. Not nearly enough, but too much.

He licked her again. This time, she felt that knowledgeable tongue teasing her clit out from underneath its hood.

Did I make that noise?

She heard the whining again.

I did make that noise.

Two fingers entered her and then they twisted in an oh-so-diabolical manner. Twisting and turning until they found a spot that had her moaning.

"Linc, baby."

"Come here."

"Kiss me."

"Stop that."

"Come here."

"Oh yeah, right there."

"Stop right now, I need your cock."

I'm blathering.

She didn't care. She was so close and it felt like she was going to fly over Niagara Falls.

"Here, baby. I'm here with you. I've got you. Give me just a little more, sweetheart. Just a little more."

What is he saying?

"Cock. Need cock."

Is he laughing?

"Give it to me, baby, then you get cock."

Leila felt the gentle scrape of teeth on her clit, and she shot over the waterfall.

"You're not carrying me, are you?"

"Pretty sure I am." Linc looked down at Leila, who was as content as a kitten sleeping next to a warm brick after drinking a bowl full of cream.

"Are you showing off your SEAL superpowers?"

"I don't know. Will I get to see you in more sexy lingerie if I say yes?"

"Probably."

"Then, yes. I'm definitely showing off my superpowers."

He bent over and pulled back the duvet, then settled her onto the bed.

"See! See there. No regular man can actually pull back the cover while he's holding a woman. You have superpowers. I'm going to tell the papers or something. Course they wouldn't be interested. Maybe Cosmo magazine. But they'd be more impressed by what you did out in the living room."

"How about you? Were you impressed?"

"Yes, I was. But do you want to know what would make me more impressed?"

Linc tried to keep a straight face as he asked. "What, honey? What would impress you more than oral sex?"

"Cock."

He lost it. He knew it had been coming, but he lost it anyway. He couldn't stop laughing.

"Hey, mister! It's not nice to laugh so hard with a naked woman in your bed. It'll give her a complex."

Linc went over and put his knee on the bed beside her and cupped her cheek. "I would never want to give you a complex. Seriously, Leila, so far, this has been one of the absolute best days of my life."

Leila slowly reached out and cupped his crotch. "Seriously, Linc. Take off your pants."

They both burst out laughing.

Linc took off his jeans in record time. He took one condom out of the drawer beside the bed and put it on top of the nightstand. He looked over at Leila, who was nodding her head.

"What?"

"Again, I find that my imagination did not do you justice."

Linc slid into the bed next to her. He crushed her to his body, and kissed her. How could someone like Leila Cloud not already have been snatched up? She was such a bright and pure spirit, with just the right bit of naughty.

He cupped her breast and brushed his thumb against her nipple, not just to give her pleasure but also because all of her felt so damn good to touch. She arched against him. She was quick to part her legs so that he could nestle against her core. He brought one of her breasts to his mouth and suckled.

The taste of her would haunt his dreams. She tasted like flowers, but more earthy and spicy. It was a taste that made him drunk. Made him want more.

"Time out."

"Huh?" he asked.

"I want to be on top."

"Works for me. Lady's choice."

Her smile got even bigger. He rolled over, careful with her so that she didn't end up with all of his weight on top of her. When she threw one of her long legs over him and tossed her head back, he thought he might have a heart attack.

"Give me that condom." She held out her hand.

He reached over and got it, then put it into her palm and she tore it open with her teeth. He almost didn't survive when she rolled it down the length of his penis. Her eyelids dropped, and she continued to hold him in her grip. "You know how you said I was pretty out in the other room?" she asked. "I mean, my girly bits?"

"Yes, I remember." Linc tried to keep his voice even, but it was tough. If she continued to circle and rub him up and down, the first use of the condom wouldn't include actual intercourse.

"Well, I want to tell you that besides being a pretty man, you have a pretty cock."

"Woman, you are going to be the death of me," Linc burst out. "Now, if you really want to make use of my pretty cock, you're going to have to take your hands off it and stop pretending I'm a joystick on some video game."

Her eyes lit up. "Joystick! That's your new nickname."

"Leila," he growled. "I like you and all, but I'm done." He picked her up by the waist, and slowly brought her down so that her wet pussy met his hungry dick.

She let out a groan. He stopped. "Are you okay?"

"God yes." She pushed his hands away. "Let me."

Slowly, she lowered herself halfway down his shaft. She hummed her pleasure, then she lifted back up, never losing their connection. She did it again.

"Leila," Linc started. He didn't know what else he was going to say, so he kept it at her name.

"You feel so good." She lifted again, but this time she twisted as she pushed down a little farther and Linc thought the top of his head would explode. He loved watching where her pussy was taking him into her body. It was such a sexy and erotic sight that it seared into his brain.

She threw back her head and dropped her hands to his thighs and slid all the way down to the root of his cock while his name came from her throat in one long moan.

She looked like some kind of ancient goddess on top of him. Strong. Powerful. Passionate. Linc slid his hands upward and caressed her rounded stomach, her ribcage, her upturned breasts, her shoulders, and then he wrapped his hands around to the back of her neck and pulled her down for a kiss.

She met him eagerly. As they kissed, Linc would press up with his hips, and Leila would push down, both of them working to find the perfect rhythm to give the other the most pleasure. The kiss became hotter as their bodies filmed with sweat.

Leila lowered her pussy down onto his cock and twisted, but that wasn't what did it. She lifted, so that they were looking each other in the eye. She squeezed her core and Linc felt his spine tingling, knowing he was close. He felt her shuddering and realized she was close, too. Then she did the thing that pushed him over the edge. She bent down and bit his lower lip, then licked.

He grabbed her hips and surged upward. She cried out his name as he pounded into her and she pulsed around him. His world exploded. He went off into the universe. A place only inhabited by Linc and Leila.

16

"Who are you? I'm sorry, but only Navy SEALs are allowed at this table."

"Shut up and pour me a beer," Linc groused as he sat down next to Jase.

"Oh, somebody's not in the bestest, greatest, rainbowdiest mood in the world. What happened, did a flower fail to bloom today?"

"You know, you can be a real asshole, you know that?" Linc said as he gave his friend an offended look.

Everybody at the table laughed, Jase the hardest, then Jase poured him a beer from the pitcher and mumbled. "Sorry, Linc. What the fuck is wrong?"

"Nothing's really wrong. It's just that Leila's three-week assignment in Quebec has turned into five weeks, and I'm getting antsy not seeing her."

Jase opened his mouth to speak, but Linc held up his hand.

"Nope, before you say it, I already know it. How in the hell can I be upset if one of her assignments has gone long, when for all she'll know I can be called out for a two-week assignment that lasts four months? What's more, I can't tell her anything about it, and I might not be able to call her for weeks at a time. I know I'm being a hypocritical asshole. I get that part."

"Well, then my work here is done."

Linc took a couple of sips of his beer and looked out the window into the harbor. "So, what's going on with you?" he asked Jase.

"Same old, same old."

"No family stories to tell? Come on, with your family there's always something," Linc prompted. "Throw me a bone. I need out of my own head."

"There's my sister's wedding coming up. I'm an usher. Her fiancé arranged for us all to get our tuxes at the same place in Duluth, two days before the big day. Sandy assures me that one will come in my size."

"All of you are going to be in Sandy's wedding? I mean, all-all of you? That's going to be a huge fucking wedding."

Jase scratched his whiskers with the back of his knuckles, a sure sign that he was getting agitated. "Tell me about it. Mom's over the moon. The fact that all of us will be together in one place, and dressed well? She feels like the moon and stars have aligned. I think that's why Sandy is doing it."

"Sandy's the oldest girl, right?"

"Yep, she was adopted after me, but she was four when I was two. We were who they started with before Mom and Dad took the show on the road."

"So, seventeen Drakos plus your parents."

"Not everyone is a Drakos. Some of my brothers and sisters were foster kids, and some were adopted when they were older, so they didn't want to change their names, but yeah, in reality, we're all Drakos."

Linc smiled. This is what he needed, some time with his friends. Hearing about Jase and his family was doing him good.

"If you're missing her so much while she's away, why don't you go home and spend some time with your folks in Minnesota?"

"Already did that last summer. Right now, I want to save all my time off to spend with Leila."

"You have it bad," Jase said with a smile.

Linc looked at his friend and saw nothing but warmth and acceptance.

"What, you're not going to give me shit?"

"Nah. From everything you've told me, and the few times she's been around and we've all hung out, I'm thinking you're one lucky bastard."

Linc sat back in his chair and grinned.

"Hey, don't get too big-headed," Jase warned. "Just because I think you might have one aspect of your life figured out, doesn't mean I'm not going to give you shit about the rest of your sorry-assed existence. Remember, we have to go get training in unmanned aerial vehicles tomorrow. Shit, I wasn't that into video games as a kid. I sure as hell don't want to be playing them now," Jase griped.

"I don't know," Linc grinned. "I've recently become more interested in video games."

"Probably comes with you babysitting your sister's kids."

"Probably not." Linc said as he took another sip of his beer. "Probably comes from somebody liking to play with my joystick."

"I AM SO sorry I'm late," Leila apologized as she scooched into the booth and took the menu from the server. "I hope you haven't been waiting long."

"Leila, don't worry about it. I haven't been waiting long at all. These days I have a lot more free time, so I make a priority of going out with friends and not always being on the clock."

Leila sat back a little in the booth and took a long look at Katherine Cole. She looked different. Not different from when they had been kidnapped. That didn't count. She looked different from when she had first met her in Syria. She looked at the pretty yellow sweater she was wearing with the cute silk blouse underneath. Leila did a quick peek and saw that she was wearing jeans and some trendy three-inch heels. Katherine actually looked pretty awesome.

"So, what's the deal? Your whole look has changed. You look happier and ten years younger than when I first met you. I want to know all of your secrets."

Katherine laughed. She reached out and clutched Leila's hand. "Everybody else has tiptoed around all the changes I've made. I've even bought a Mercedes AMG convertible. I've heard the term *mid-life crisis* whispered behind my back."

"Well, hot damn, sister. Look at you go."

"I also stepped down from the CEO position."

Leila frowned. "Is that something you wanted to do, or did someone force it on you?"

"Oh no, this was my idea. When I created this company, I set it up that I could only be terminated because of criminal acts. That will not happen, so if they don't like how I'm doing things, they can piss off."

Leila laughed again, then thanked the waiter as he

brought her water, bread, and butter. He asked if they were ready to order and since neither of them were, they asked him to come back.

"We better get this figured out, then we can catch up some more," Katherine said as she picked up her menu. "I recommend everything. I have not had a poor meal since coming here."

It didn't take long for Leila to settle on the ahi tuna, and Katherine chose chicken and rice.

"So why did you step down as CEO?"

"I'm sixty-seven. I've devoted over forty years to this company, and before my husband died, I had something they now call work-life balance. When you met me in Syria, I was normally working sixty to seventy hours a week. I have two grandchildren who hardly recognize me, but sure as hell recognize their other grandmother." Katherine took a sip of water. "Well, I'll tell you, our time in Syria was a wake-up call. I've got a do-over, and I'm making the most of it."

Leila frowned. How much had she changed since Syria? Except for dating Linc, and not taking iffy translation assignments, her life was pretty much the same as it always was.

"What has you thinking so hard?" Katherine asked.

"I'm trying to think if I have made any life-altering decisions since Syria. I'm not sure that I have and I'm thirty-one."

"And there's your answer. You're thirty-six years younger than I am. You have your whole life ahead of you to live, love, and try new things. It's going to be so exciting."

Their server came with their food, and Leila dug in.

She was still pondering the do-over revelation when Katherine brought up Elijah.

"I was sorry to hear that he passed. I actually heard about it from my assistant, Annie. She sets Google alerts for me about people I'm interested in. I have one on you too, of course."

Leila nodded. "Elijah and my dad go way back; he was actually my godfather."

"Oh, honey, seeing him dragged away like that in Syria, and then having him die, must have been heart-wrenching."

"It was. But like my dad always said, Elijah always enjoyed knowing he was making the world a better place."

"And he did. Ultimately, he got those prisoners free."

Leila frowned. "What are you talking about? The CIA took back the diamonds. They were never delivered. How could the prisoners be free?"

"It was announced on CNN a month ago that our ambassador had negotiated for their release. I'd just assumed that somehow Elijah's plan had worked, even after everything that had happened."

"No, it couldn't have. I was the only oth—" Leila stopped herself. It wasn't that she didn't trust Katherine, it was just that her father was FBI and her godfather used to be CIA; she knew better than to share too many secrets.

"Honey, you don't have to tell me anything."

Leila smiled at that. "I appreciate you saying that. Actually, that's a time I'd actually prefer to forget."

"I can't."

"Oh no, do you have nightmares?" Leila asked.

"No. Not at all. You just pop up in my mind a lot. I couldn't have made it without you. I flew to DC to come and see you. When we parted in Syria, I never had a chance to tell you thank you for what you'd done for me. Thank you, Leila. Thank you for saving my life."

Leila felt her cheeks heat.

Is this how Linc feels every time I thank him? A little uncomfortable, but kind of proud?

"Katherine. I want to thank you. There is no other person I would have preferred being stuck in a hole with."

LEILA HIT the garage door opener and slid her car next to Linc's truck. It still felt odd, not only having a key to someone else's house, but the garage door opener. She would have thought it was rushing the relationship, except the one time she showed up and he wasn't there she had no way to get in. She'd checked her messages and found a text had come in when she was already en route, saying that he had overnight training and would not be there. Linc gave her the key and the remote after that.

She got out and popped the trunk. Linc was already out the garage door from the kitchen and headed her way.

"You know I'm the same person who put my luggage in my car, don't you?" she asked as he plucked her suitcase, backpack, and laptop case out of the trunk.

"You're funny." He smiled down at her. He then followed her up the steps and into his kitchen. As soon as the garage door was closed, he put the laptop bag on the counter, dropped the luggage, and grabbed her.

She'd been waiting for this. Waiting far too fricking long for this. Linc bent and settled his lips on hers, enticing her to open up. She did, needing his taste. That first thrust of his tongue made her tighten her grip on him so that she wouldn't fall down. His hand was up the back of her sweater and her skin heated wherever he touched. Her bra felt itchy as they sampled and savored one another after being parted for six weeks.

He pulled back.

"Have you eaten?"

"Don't care about food," she muttered.

"Leila, answer me. Have you eaten?"

"Had a donut this morning when I went to the corner to grab coffee."

"Dinner first, fucking second, then we can make love."

"No," she whined. "I haven't gotten to see you and touch you in six entire weeks."

"Remember this moment and maybe you'll think about stopping off and getting something to eat from now on. You need to take better care of yourself, Leila. I worry about you."

She plopped her forehead onto his chest. "I so should have lied."

Linc laughed, then picked up her luggage and she followed him.

"Linc, you don't always have to carry my stuff," she said again.

"I don't carry your purse," he said as he put her bags in his bedroom, then headed to his office with her laptop bag.

"I'm being serious."

"It's my job to carry your luggage or the groceries inside. If my father ever saw me letting you haul things or opening your own door while I was around, he'd give me 'the look.' I never want to receive 'the look.'

"You know, you haven't talked much about your mom and dad. I've heard everything about your brothers and sisters. You've got to fill me in on them. They sound great."

"George Hart is my stepdad, and he is great. I'd go so far as to say he is wonderful. My mom loves him, and he adores my mother. He treats her like she is fine china. He's this big, gruff guy who used to drive trucks and he still goes ice fishing. Now he owns his own towing company. He's still big and gruff, but whenever mom's near, he's a perfect gentleman. Me and my brothers definitely caught on to that."

"You're kind of describing my dad as well. Not the big and gruff part, but definitely the gentlemanly part. It's funny, I've never seen my dad with his FBI persona, but I got to see Elijah with his a couple of times. Makes me really want to see my dad's, you know?"

Linc laughed. "I guess so," he said as he left the office, where he put her case on his desk.

"So, which do you want? I can cook you dinner, or we can order in."

"Let's go for home-cooked, as long as I can help."

"I love mutual participation activities with you, Ms. Cloud."

17

LINC LOVED SEEING LEILA IN HIS HOME. SHE LOOKED GOOD there. Hers was nice, but a little more sterile. He was surprised she didn't have more pictures of her travels on the wall. When he mentioned it, she showed him some picture albums, and said she always planned to, but never got around to it.

It didn't take him long to figure out she'd never really built herself a real nest. A place to come home to. Instead, that was her parent's house, but her apartment was nothing more than a place to rest between translation assignments.

She sat down on her corner of his couch, propped her plate up on her knees and used chopsticks like a pro to eat her Mongolian beef and noodles.

"So, how was your time in Quebec?"

"Boring. The people were nice, but the meetings were jaw-droppingly boring. I outlined the great American novel in my head during the first week of meetings."

"What's your book about?"

"It starts out about a strapping young man from

Minnesota, who leaves when he is eighteen to find his fortune and fame in Hollywood. But he gets waylaid at a diner in Texas by the name of Dusty."

"Hate to tell you this, but there's a problem with your book right from the start. There is no way your hero would travel from Minnesota, down to Texas, then over to Southern California, just doesn't make sense. Too much wear and tear on the tires."

Linc tucked into his spicy shrimp and sighed with pleasure.

"I just decided that my strapping young man wanted to find his fortune in the oil fields of Texas."

Linc nodded. "Now that makes sense. You may proceed."

She continued to weave a fantastical tale of Maurice and Dusty and their lusty adventures as he worked the oilfields during the day, but came back to her doublewide every night.

"So, what makes you think this will be a best-seller?"

"I'm pretty sure I can write a good sex scene." He watched as she picked up a long noodle and sucked it down, her cheeks hollowing out. He forgot what they were talking about.

"Linc, are you done eating? Because I am."

He stood up in a daze and took her plate from her and dropped all the dirty dishes into his sink, not even bothering to soak them.

"Let me change," she said as he stalked over to her.

"Honey, I don't care what kind of bits of froth, silk and lace you have waiting for me in that suitcase of yours. I don't have time for you to change." Leila let out a sharp squeak when he put her over his shoulder and started toward his bedroom. She kept squirming but made no verbal protests. Her wiggles were driving him wild, and he didn't know if he could make it to the bedroom.

"Stop that," he commanded as he slapped her ass.

"No, if you're going to do that," she panted. "Why would I stop squirming?"

He swatted her butt again, but this time he left his hand on it and squeezed. She had a great ass. He couldn't wait to see it in his bed again.

"Put me down," she demanded.

"As you wish," he smiled as she slipped down the front of him until they were nose to nose. He gave in and kissed her. It was a slow and languid hello, between two lovers who knew one another but had been parted long enough that they needed to reinforce their connection.

So good. So, fucking good.

"Leila, touching you was my dream. But right now? Having you in my arms. This is perfection."

He felt her body tremble. "Sheesh, with words like that, we're going to have to skip the fucking and go straight to the making love part of our program," she whispered.

"It's true. I've missed you so goddamned bad. It was like I was missing a limb."

"Let's talk about the two weeks you were gone before that. We didn't get to have phone sex during that time, or anything." She breathed the words into his ear.

The hot air of her breath made his cock even harder.

"Don't get me wrong, I've become a fan of phone sex with you. Only you. But not tonight. Tonight, I don't have to dream, because here you are."

She settled herself down onto the side of the bed, and he pulled off her coral sweater and tossed it over his head.

Then he smirked when he saw the padded bra. "For me?" he asked.

"I wasn't sure if we were going out to dinner tonight or what, but a lady does not have her nipples out and proud for the world to see. My mother would have a fit if she ever saw that."

"That's fine by me. I like the idea of all your beauty being my very own secret treasure." He unhooked the back of her bra, then drew it down her arms. Soon the utilitarian garment also went over his head, and he was back to pleasuring her breasts, and doing everything possible to drive her insane.

"I need your slacks off. Now." He found the fastening for her tailored pants on her hip, and he unzipped them. He took off her pants and panties at the same time.

"So unfair. Why are you always dressed, and I'm always naked?"

"Good planning."

Linc traced a circle around her belly button with his tongue, then leisurely licked her all the way up her body until he kissed her trembling lips. Kissing Leila was a dream. Her lips were so pillowy soft, and when they rounded to suck his tongue in deep, his cock pulsed.

He let go of her and pulled off his shirt, and got out of his jeans in record time.

"Ohh, naked. I like naked."

He didn't have time for talking. He turned her body so that her legs hung over the side of the bed. He grabbed a condom out of the nightstand, and put it on, then took one of her long, beautiful legs and slid it over his shoulder.

"Linc?"

It was the first time he had ever heard even the

slightest sound of trepidation in her voice while they were in bed together.

"It's going to be fine. It's all you. You're always in charge. You tell me if it gets to be too much, okay?"

Wide brown eyes looked up at him with total trust. "Okay."

Linc kissed the foot that rested on his shoulder, then pushed her other leg out a little further to widen her, just a little more for his viewing pleasure.

He took a quick look at her face, and he didn't see fear or discomfort, so he continued. Continuing to hold her right foot in his hand, he used his left hand to guide his cock into her wet pussy. In one long stroke, he sank to the root.

Leila gasped. Again, he looked up at her face to check on her. She was smiling. God knows he was doing an internal little happy dance.

He pulled out slowly, watching as her flesh tried to keep hold of him. It was as if every part of her body wanted him, as much as he wanted her. He pushed back in slowly.

Again and again, he continued with the rhythm, continuing to watch between where they were merged and then back up at her flushed face. Soon, it was time to add something more to the mix.

"Give me your hand."

"Huh?"

"You're left-handed. I want your left hand, baby."

She raised her hand, and he kissed her palm. Then he guided it down to her slick pussy.

"Touch yourself."

Her eyes went wide. "What?" she exclaimed.

Gone was dreamy Leila, back was spitfire Leila.

"You've told me how you've pleasured yourself before. You touched yourself in Quebec, didn't you?"

She stared up at him.

"Didn't you, beauty? Didn't you brush your hand across your gorgeous tits, then let it wander down your belly until you slid your fingers into your slick folds?"

It took a moment, but she nodded.

"Did you touch your clit?" he asked as he continued to thrust slowly in and pull slowly out.

"Y-yes," she stuttered.

"Show me," he coaxed. "Let me watch."

He watched as she took her middle finger and pulled back the hood of her clit. She sucked in a quick breath of surprise. It was like she wasn't expecting the spark of her own touch.

"Keep going."

Linc was holding on by the skin of his teeth. Trying to maintain a steady rhythm, while he got to watch her touch herself, was damn near impossible.

She started to circle that pink, swollen morsel and he stopped, just kept himself rooted inside her as his world narrowed down to her graceful finger touching her delicate clit. She kept circling and circling, then she pressed down. Hard. And she lifted up, pressing her pelvis tight against his. Waking him up to the fact that he was falling down on the job.

Linc picked up the speed of his strokes. In and out, twisting and moving until he found just the right spot inside her channel that had her gasping.

"Yeah. There, baby. There."

As he made sure to drag the tip of his cock against her g-spot, she pressed harder against her clit. Her entire body blushed, and beads of sweat formed at her temples.

Linc felt like there was rocket fuel churning in his lower back, a fire waiting to be let loose. He stroked in and out, then let her foot drop to the bed, and then brushed her finger away, so that he could touch and feel that part of her that gave her so much pleasure.

"Harder."

He didn't know if she meant his cock, or if she wanted a stronger touch on her clit, but he supplied both.

Leila practically howled as her orgasm overtook her, and he thanked God, because he couldn't hold back a moment longer. One more surge, and he felt her pussy clasp him tight. Hold him close. His release was unlike anything he had ever felt before.

It was pure beauty.

18

"YOU SEEM PRETTY HAPPY WITH YOURSELF THESE DAYS," Grant Cloud said as they left Nordstrom's. "As a matter of fact, I don't think I've ever seen you happier, and that includes the time that you got your master's and the job offer with the Turkish consulate here in DC."

Leila grinned.

"That's only because I am happier. And it's not because we found the perfect summer coat for mom's birthday."

"Honey, I didn't think it was that. I thought it was because you were going out to lunch with your old man."

Leila laughed and grabbed her father's arm. They continued to wind their way down the street, managing not to run into any of the other pedestrians. Her father had that knack of getting people to step out of his way. The same knack that Linc did.

"So, have you decided where you wanted me to take you?"

"And if I told you I wanted to go to the American Girl Restaurant?"

She could actually feel her dad shudder.

"Then I would say, let's go."

"Oh my God, Dad. You're the best. It wasn't until I was about sixteen that I looked back on our trip to that restaurant and realized you might not have had as much fun as I did."

Her dad stopped walking. "Leila, I did have as much fun as you did. Watching you bring your doll to the store, and having her put in her highchair and the two of us eating tater tots, is one of my fondest memories. Your big brown eyes were wider than I had ever seen them. It was like I took you to Disneyland and Sea World at the same time."

"It was pretty cool, and my dolly, Polly, loved it."

They continued their walk down the sidewalk.

She felt the first raindrop fall when they were at the crosswalk. "I was going to say that it might be nice to hit that restaurant with the outdoor seating four blocks down, but not so much anymore," Leila winced.

I should have brought an umbrella.

By the time they'd crossed the street, it was a real downpour. Nothing new for Washington DC in May.

Why didn't I bring a fucking umbrella!?

"Honey, are you okay?" her dad asked.

She gulped. "No. I don't like it raining on me anymore. I don't like it, Dad."

"Shit." Grant Cloud took off his overcoat and held it over his daughter's head. Leila felt like she could breathe again. "If I thought it was just going to blow over, I'd say we could just stop in one of these stores." He glanced up into the sky. "It looks like it's here to stay."

Leila tried to concentrate on what he was saying and

not the way her wet hair felt, and the sound of the raindrops falling on his coat, right over her head.

"It's only two blocks this way, before we get to the parking garage. Can you make it, sweetheart?"

Leila gritted her teeth. "Sure."

It was a blur as her dad hustled her down the blocks to the bank building where his car was parked. When they went through the revolving door and made it into the enormous lobby, she was almost in tears. Her dad pulled her into his arms.

"You never went to see anyone. No counselling, right?"

She shook her head as she burrowed closer.

"You are now. You get that, right?"

She nodded her head.

Leila didn't know how long they stood like that, drowned rats in the middle of one of the biggest and oldest banks in DC, but nobody gave them any guff. She wondered if her dad had flashed his FBI badge to keep them at bay.

When she finally pulled her shit together, she took a step back. "I'm better now."

"You sure?"

"Well, I'm not up for tater tots at American Girl. But I sure could use a grilled cheese made by mom."

Her dad laughed.

They walked to the bank of elevators, and he pressed the floor to where his car was parked. When they stepped out of the elevators, Leila could see her dad's car. He'd backed it in as usual. Linc did the same thing, something about an easy exit. *Men.*

Her dad still kept his arm around her, his coat and the Nordstrom package in his other hand. "I really am all right. I hardly ever lose it like that anymore," she assured her father.

He turned to her as they stood in front of his car. "I don't care if it only happens once a year. You still need to get in and see someone. I'm going to call our in-house psychologist and get you a referral. It's been five months, Leila. The more you let this fester, the worse it's going to get."

"Okay, I promise."

"That's my girl. Now let me put this into the trunk, then I'll open your door."

"Dad, I don't have a broken arm."

"What's the rule?" he teased.

She watched as her dad went around the back to put the Nordstrom bag and box into the trunk. She looked up when she heard some asshole driving too fast in the parking garage. Since she was with her dad, she didn't yell out the speed limit like she might have if she were alone. Her dad came up to her and started to open the door, when a black panel van skidded to a stop right in front of their car.

Two men, all dressed in black, with ski masks on their faces, jumped out. Before she knew what was happening, her dad had pushed her behind him, so hard that she fell onto her hands and knees onto the cement.

She heard a shot fired and screamed.

"Dad!"

Two more shots were fired. They were deafening.

Her dad fell backward on top of her. Their car passenger door was slammed shut. Over her dad's shoulder, she could see one man with the ski mask pulling at her dad's arm, trying to take him away from her.

"No! You can't have him!" she screamed. She pulled her father back on top of her.

The terrorist continued to pull on her father's arm, and she wrapped her arms around his chest and felt blood. It only made her squeeze harder.

"Let go!" the man said. He had an accent. She tried to place it, but stopped thinking as another man came up and pulled on her dad's other arm. She was not going to win this fight. She screamed for help.

That was when she saw a gun under the car to the right. It had to be her dad's. She let go of her dad, aimed, and shot.

"Bitch!"

She saw one of them try to hit her, but she ducked down behind her dad's broad shoulders, and he missed. That was when she heard the yelling. Lots of yelling.

People were coming.

The terrorists must have heard it too because they gave up trying to kidnap her dad, and ran back to the van. She didn't care if they got away. There was too much blood. Just too much blood.

Linc got to the hospital as fast as he could. Gideon had found a way to get him on a plane in less than forty-five minutes after Leila's call. Not only did Linc go, but Jase went with him.

When he got to the hospital floor that Leila had told him to go, he was met by police. They would only let Linc go to the waiting room, and even that had a guard in front of it. The room was filled with solemn-faced men and women who wanted to be there for Miray and Leila

Cloud. But it was obvious these were just co-workers of her dad, not friends and family. He hated seeing Leila and her mother alone like that.

He looked around for Tessa and Jackie, but they weren't there. He vaguely remembered that Leila's friend Tessa was in Tahoe, but he didn't know why Jackie wasn't there. He crossed the room fast, and knelt in front of the two women, and put a hand on each of their knees. Mrs. Cloud didn't look up, but Leila did. She grasped his hand in both of hers, like it was a lifeline.

"You came."

"Of course, I did."

The man sitting next to Leila got up to stand next to a window and Linc sat down beside her, so he could wrap his arm around her. She shoved her face into his neck, and he felt the wet of her tears. Not even after all the shit that came down in Syria had she been like this.

He looked up and saw Miray Cloud looking at him; she had a sort of smile on her lips. "How is your husband?" he asked.

"We don't know yet. He's still in surgery."

Linc nodded.

Leila gripped him tighter.

He saw Jase walk into the room. He must have passed inspection. Linc gave him a chin tilt, and he walked over and put his ear next to Linc's mouth.

"Can you find out her dad's status? These suits have to know the truth, and these ladies can't handle not knowing it."

Jase stood up and nodded.

He walked back out of the waiting room.

It was ten minutes later that a silver-haired man in a

suit, with his tie askew, came over and took the seat that was immediately vacated next to Miray Cloud.

"Paul," she exclaimed. "Nobody will tell me what's going on. Grant has been in surgery for over four hours. Please, just tell me what's going on."

"He was shot only once. In the chest. But Leila told you that. Going in, they didn't think they were going to be able to repair one of his lungs, but they were going to try. His heart wasn't hit, so that was good news."

"What about the other shots I heard?" Leila asked.

"His gun had been discharged three times, and you told us you had fired one shot. That means that your dad took the other two shots. That's probably what saved him and you from being kidnapped."

"Kidnapped?" Miray gasped. "Why would someone want to kidnap my family?"

"We're not sure," Paul answered.

"They weren't trying to kidnap me, they kept trying to pull dad out of my arms so that they could take him."

"Leila, I know you've wanted to be here for your mother, and I can understand it. But I would really like you to make your statement now."

"To the police?"

"No, to Agent Carlson of the FBI..." Paul pointed up to a tall, good-looking African American man who had a kind smile.

"Okay."

Linc knew she hadn't even realized she was still clutching his hand. He turned to Paul, whoever he was. "Can I go with her? I'm Lincoln Hart, her boyfriend. I'm also Special Operations with the United States Navy, out of Little Creek."

"S.E.A.L.?" Paul asked.

Linc nodded.

"That's fine." He turned to Agent Carlson. "Let her boyfriend go along with her."

"You'll stay with mom?" she asked Paul.

"Absolutely."

She gave Paul a grateful smile, then lifted one hand away from Linc's, and held his hand normally as they followed Agent Carlson down the hall.

19

Linc watched Leila's every move as she started talking to the agent. He hated to see her trembling. He hated to hear her voice so shaky. And it about killed him when started to cry as she described pulling her dad down against her so they wouldn't pull him away from her.

"I know this is difficult for you, Ms. Cloud," Agent Carlson said. Another agent had come in with them, Agent Gilder. She didn't say anything, she just took notes and observed.

"No, I'm fine. I want to give you as much information as possible so you can get these bastards who tried to kidnap my dad."

"That's what I want to go over with you again." The agent smiled as he pushed the cup of lukewarm coffee toward her. "You heard three shots before you shot your dad's pistol, is that correct?"

"Yes."

"Was it one shot, pause and then two shots? Or was it

two shots, pause and then one shot? Do you remember the sequence?"

Linc watched as she gnawed at her lower lip. "Why does that make a difference?"

"I'm just trying to get a full picture of what happened."

"There was one shot...then another shot," she looked up at him, her face suffused with confusion. "Then there was a third shot. I don't know. I just don't know. All I remember was that Dad was putting Mom's present into the trunk. I heard the screeching tires and thought what an asshole, then Dad closed the trunk, walked past me so he could open the passenger door for me to get in. But before I could, I saw the van skid to a halt in front of us, and two men dressed in black with ski masks jumped out. The next thing I knew, I was on my hands and knees on the cement floor of the garage. I didn't even know they had guns until I heard the shots."

"You were found on your back, with your father lying on his back on top of you, how did that happen?" the agent asked.

"I'm not sure. I think I tried to get up after I heard the shots. I was worried for Dad. Then it was like he was shoved back against me, and we both toppled backward. I think he was trying to protect me."

"I'm sure he was." Agent Carlson nodded. "Can you tell me how you got your father's gun?"

"It was after they tried to pull him off me. One of them leaned down and grabbed Dad's arm and pulled."

"Can you describe him?"

"He had brown eyes, and the gloves he was wearing didn't reach the sleeves of his shirt. He was brown like me. So, more Hispanic or Middle Eastern, not African American."

Detective Carlson nodded and continued to write notes. What else did you notice about him, any tattoos, distinguishing marks?

Leila shook her head. "No. Nothing."

"Okay then, when he tried to pull your dad away from you, what happened then? I grabbed hold of Dad with both of my arms and locked one hand over my wrist real tight. I wasn't going to let them take him. There was already so much blood on Dad's chest."

"You're doing good. Then what happened?"

"The other man came over and started to help pull Dad away. That's when I started to scream for help. I knew I wasn't going to win. I was frantic. I was screaming, and struggling, then I saw Dad's gun under the car beside me, and I grabbed it with my right hand. As soon as I had a good hold on it, I let go of Dad entirely, and I shot at the first guy. I knew I'd missed before I even took the shot because the gun slipped with all the blood on my hands. Before I could take another shot, the guy tried to hit me in the face, but I ducked down behind Dad. I fucked up, I should have taken another shot."

"Stop it, Leila," Linc whispered as he took her hand. "You handled yourself great. You and your dad are both alive. That's a win."

"Your boyfriend is right. Your dad is alive because of the steps you took."

"Can I go out and be with my mom now?"

"Yes," Agent Carlson said. "Can we get you another cup of coffee before you go back out there?"

"Is that what that was in the cup?" Leila teased.

"I'll go send Jase on a Starbucks run, sweetheart. Let's go get you back with your mom."

LINC WAS FINALLY a little bit comfortable. It wasn't because the couch in the waiting room was comfortable. Hell no, they made sure that the cushions came from a quarry. But having Leila lying with her head resting on his thigh, made this whole thing somewhat bearable. He looked over at Miray and saw that Paul's wife had come in and she was doing better, but still, it was now going on eight hours of surgery. Leila's hands were still coated with her father's blood and she didn't want to wash it off. She didn't say it out loud, but Linc knew it was because if he died, she didn't want to lose that last little connection.

He pushed the hair off her cheek and stroked it back down over her shoulder, then Jase caught his eye. Linc looked up and saw that a woman in scrubs had just walked into the waiting room and she was looking around.

"I'm looking for Grant Cloud's family?"

Linc helped right Leila into a sitting position, then nodded toward the doctor. "She has some information, baby."

Leila tried to scramble off the couch too fast and almost tripped, but Linc steadied her. They went over to stand next to her mother, who grabbed Leila's hand.

"He's going to need to be in the intensive care unit for a couple of days. I was able to save half of his right lung, but the bad news is the bullet ended up lodged in the anterior aspect of the subepicardial right ventricular outflow tract."

"English," Paul requested quietly.

"Sorry, I'm tired," the surgeon apologized. "Look, that means that the bullet was lodged in a part of his heart. We were able to repair the damage and stop the bleeding. We want to monitor him for about a week, but we suspect that there won't be any additional bleeding and at that point we can recommend outpatient procedures. His lung is also going to be a problem, but we can go over that later."

"He's going to live?" Miray asked.

The surgeon took off her operating cap, revealing gleaming gold hair. "Yes, Mrs. Cloud he's going to live, and in my opinion, he will thrive. Especially if he is willing to listen to his doctors."

"Oh, he'll listen," Miray promised. "He'll listen. Can I go see him now?" She turned to Leila. "Both of us? Can we both go see him?"

"He'll be transferred from post-op to the ICU in probably twenty minutes. I'll make sure a nurse comes down and gets you as soon as possible, all right?"

"Yes, Doctor. Definitely all right. God bless you."

Linc made sure to keep his arms around both Leila and her mother as they both looked ready to collapse, even though they had blinding smiles on their faces.

"THEY SLEEPING?" Jase asked as Linc came downstairs.

"Yeah," Linc nodded. "She's up there cuddled under the covers with her mom. I keep imagining Leila as a little girl, sneaking in to sleep in her parents' bed when there was a storm."

Linc sat down at the kitchen table where Jase had a bottle of bourbon set out for him. Linc poured himself two fingers, then rolled the glass between his hands.

"Did you see the way she flinched when it started to rain?"

Jase nodded.

"She told me about the flashback she had today when she was out with her father. He helped her through the whole thing. Kept ahold of her, hugged her tight, right there in the middle of that big bank lobby off Sixteenth until she got herself back together. Then he bullied her into agreeing to go to counselling."

"I'm really liking this guy."

"And I know that in the back of her mind, that even if he pulls through, she's going to be worried that he'll throw a clot a month later and die, like Elijah did."

"Fuck," Jase said right before he drank down his whole shot of bourbon.

"Yeah," Linc agreed. He took a sip of his bourbon then started rolling his glass between his two hands again.

"What?" Jase asked.

"I overheard Grant's boss talking."

"Paul?"

"Yeah. Paul. He was talking to Carlson, the guy who took Leila's statement. Right now they have everyone in their office going through Grant's old case files to see what might ping, because there is nothing that he's currently working on that could have brought on this attack."

"But he's high up, right?"

"Yeah. I get where you're going. They also talked about Grant's subordinates, and what cases they're working on. There are two that seem possible, but both are homegrown militia groups, so Leila seeing someone who wasn't Caucasian knocks that possibility down a bit."

"Linc, you're going to have to spell it out for me. I'm tired. I did an extra circuit around the obstacle course to show young Landon Kelly that being young isn't all it's cracked up to be."

"It's just that I was listening to Leila give a step-by-step accounting of what happened. I'm not totally convinced they were after her dad. I think they could have been after her."

Jase sat up straighter in his seat and pushed aside the bottle of bourbon.

"How are you seeing that?"

"She kept thinking they were trying to take her dad away from her. Like they wanted to kidnap him. Maybe it was that they wanted to pull him off her so they could take *her*."

Jace's brown eyes roamed around the kitchen as if they were looking for someplace peaceful to land. Finally, they came back to look at him. "Are you thinking this goes back to Syria?"

"Well, I don't think she made enemies while working as an interpreter for the Quebec Symphony Orchestra. I mean, I know there was some infighting between some of the various international performers, but I don't think anyone wants to kidnap her."

"So it's Vugar."

"That's what I think. And that fucking Jerry Earnst didn't give one flying fuck about him; all he seemed to care about was those diamonds and probably making sure that he didn't get any blowback from the phone being a piece of shit."

Jase nodded. "I can see that."

Linc got up from the table and started pacing. He pulled at his bottom lip, then turned and did another circuit around the kitchen.

"But what makes this whole idea useless, is that we left Syria five months ago. Why in the hell would Vugar be after Leila now? Not sooner?"

"Maybe he didn't know where she was?" Jase suggested.

"That's bullshit. The way Leila explained it to me, the guy had her resume and her childhood immunization records with him. He would have known where to find her. So why now?"

"That's a pretty big hole in your theory, Linc."

He sat back down and picked up his glass of bourbon and took another sip. Then he looked at his watch.

"Don't do it," Jase warned.

"I'm not going to call him. I'm just going to send him a text."

Jase rolled his eyes.

Linc pulled out his phone and took a good five minutes to compose a text to Gideon before he pressed send.

"I don't feel comfortable going through their refrigerator for food. Wanna order pizza?" Linc asked.

His phone rang. He looked down and saw Gideon's number and he smiled. "You know what I like on my pizza, you place the order."

20

Linc had spent two hours at the hospital with Miray and Leila already that morning before leaving them there so that he could go back to the Cloud home and set up for a meeting. Traffic was tough, so Jase was already in front of his laptop with Gideon and Kostya on the screen by the time Linc sat down behind Grant's desk.

Linc felt a little antsy getting Kostya involved, knowing he was blowing through Navy resources on his girlfriend, but Kostya nipped that in the bud right from the get-go.

"You're not using Navy resources. You and a few of your friends are getting together on a call because they're concerned about your woman. Gideon pulled me in because I have one or two friends over at Langley, that I *would* and *have*, trusted with my life. One of them has moved up in the world, so I called her before the sun was up this morning."

"And?" Linc asked.

"I mentioned Vugar and Syria to her, and she said she'd call me back. Fifteen minutes later, when I got a call from an unknown satellite phone, I picked it up. It was

Caryn. She wanted me to give her as much info as I could on Vugar. She wasn't aware of everything that had happened in Syria."

"Aw, fuck," Linc said. "How high up is she?"

"High enough that it should have hit her desk, unless somebody destroyed the intel before it made the rounds," Kostya said. "High enough that she was a hairsbreadth away from having our entire team, Sam Phelps, Katherine Cole, and her secretary Annie, and Leila pulled into CIA headquarters to go over everything in minute detail."

"Why didn't she go that route?" Jase asked.

Gideon raised his hand. "I'll take this one for two hundred, Alex."

"Fuck that, this is the double jeopardy finale question," Kostya said.

"Okay, I bet it all and my answer is, 'She thinks Vugar has a spy at Langley who could be her level or above,'" Linc answered.

"You lose, you didn't answer in the form of a question." Jase nudged him with his shoulder.

Kostya nodded. "But if you had, you would be the official winner of this fucked up game." "Obviously, from Leila's report alone it was clear that Vugar had information that he had most likely received from CIA headquarters. Add to the fact that he knew when and where to attack that day—and to grab Elijah—someone had to have handed him the exact blueprint of what was planned that day."

"That still doesn't give us anything to go on regarding Leila's attempted kidnapping."

"Caryn's going to come out to visit with you, Jase, and Leila."

"No," Linc said vehemently. "If there's a spy out there,

and they're as high up as Caryn thinks they are, then I don't want any CIA agent within a hundred miles of Leila."

"I told you. She can be trusted."

"Kostya, he's right," Gideon broke in. "I told you all about the stingray capabilities. You know that Homeland Security, FBI and the CIA. have all had this technology in their pocket. Not miniaturized, but available to them. The only thing stopping them from using it on people here in the US is all the laws that are in place to stop them. They need a ream of paper signed in blood by a judge before they can get a warrant, and even then, it can only be used narrowly."

"Yeah?" Kostya said.

"But whoever the spy is at Langley knows about the tech, and he probably was on board when I handed over the correct patches to fix Leila's phone. I'm sure they've got it miniaturized by now, and Vugar's spy won't ask for permission to use it to its fullest capabilities."

"Well hell, if that's all you're worried about, don't be. Caryn called me from her husband's satellite phone. The one they keep in the family safe to be used when you're really feeling paranoid."

"If I worked for the CIA, I'd be using that phone day in and day out," Jase muttered.

"Okay then. She's smart," Gideon nodded. "Got it."

"I'll arrange it so Caryn travels without any kind of tech, and she rides with me and Gideon. How does that sound?"

"Still not good," Linc said as he shook his head. "What's she planning on doing for Leila? Seems to me she wants information about Vugar for her agency, and she'll want to use Leila's knowledge to figure out who might be the spy. Hell, she's probably salivating at the thought of using Leila as bait, so Vugar attempts another kidnapping. Then she can catch Vugar and trace him back to the spy."

"She wouldn't do that. Kostya told us she's on board to help," Jase protested.

Linc continued to stare at his lieutenant through the video screen, refusing to break eye contact.

"Linc, you're almost beginning to think like a paranoid Russian. Must be because you grew up surrounded by so much snow." Kostya sat back in his chair and gave Gideon a quick glance, who just shrugged. Kostya turned back to look at Linc.

"Linc. We're not one hundred percent sure that Leila was the target, so this could all be a moot point, agreed?"

Linc nodded.

"But if this is real, it's ninety-nine-point nine percent sure that it's Vugar who's after her, agreed?"

Linc nodded.

"Do you know why? What would she have that his CIA spy wouldn't have? She was just an add-on to this mission. She was just supposed to smooth things over."

"Elijah was her godfather. He and her dad went way back. I've never asked her to tell me all the details of the operation, because it's not right. Same way she doesn't ask about my job."

"I like her more and more." Jase grinned.

"It's possible that there is something that Vugar wants and can only get it from her, especially now that Elijah has died," Kostya went on.

"Why didn't they try to kidnap him when he was first back in the States?" Jase asked.

Linc looked over at Jase and frowned. "I thought I told you Elijah came back from Syria with a traumatic brain injury. He was very low functioning. He couldn't have told them his own name."

"Damn. Your girl's been through a lot."

"So, we agree. She has some information that Vugar wants," Kostya summarized. "And Linc, I hate to say this, but I think you're right. If Caryn saw a way to take down Vugar and out the spy at Langley, she would gladly use Leila as bait."

"Depending on what the information is, we could just email it to Vugar," Jase said hopefully. "That'd be the end of everything."

"Drakos, you're now relegated to the children's table of this conversation," Gideon said with a warning look.

"Linc," Kostya started. "There's still hope that this is something that we can count on Caryn's help for, and she won't want to use Leila. But the only way we'll know is to talk to Leila."

"LEILA, did you see how well he was doing? Did you? His grip was so strong." Miray was looking so much better than she had a day and a half ago when they'd been waiting for her father to get out of surgery. Even after seeing him in recovery, neither she nor her mom had been reassured. It was like Elijah all over again.

Today was better.

Today there had been a glimmer of the normal Grant Edward Cloud.

"I saw *anne*. I saw." She pushed a plate of eggplant parmigiana in front of her. "Now eat. You haven't eaten since you rushed to the hospital."

Her mother actually looked down at the food and

smiled. This, too, was a first since her dad had been shot. "I can't eat all of this. It's enough for three people," Miray protested.

"Then eat a third of it. The rest we can put in the fridge for leftovers, or Jace will eat it."

Miray looked up and smiled at the two big men who were sitting in front of their own dinners that Linc had picked up from Adolpho's. It was one of her mom's favorite restaurants.

"Mrs. Cloud, I have your back." Jase looked up from his plate and winked at her.

"Jase, I told you, call me Miray."

"Okay, Miray. Now I know why you rave about this place; the food is spectacular."

Miray leaned forward, smiling brightly. "It is, isn't it? Grant takes me there at least once a month. *Bebek*, we should have gotten some for your father, so he could have it tomorrow."

Leila closed her eyes for just a moment, then opened them again. "Mom, they will not let dad have rich food like this for quite a while. My guess is they're going to be giving you a whole new diet that he'll need."

"You're right, Leila. After the hospital tomorrow, we can go to the grocery store."

Leila sat down in her spot between Linc and her mom. "We'll talk about it, okay? In the meantime, let's have a nice meal and maybe a good night's sleep, okay?"

"That sounds good."

WHEN SHE WAS sure her mom was settled in for the night, she joined Linc and Jase at the kitchen table.

"Bourbon?" she asked as Linc got up and pulled out a seat for her.

"Your dad has a well-supplied home office," Linc murmured as he kissed her temple and pushed in her chair.

"I forgot he keeps a bottle in his office."

"What's on offer tonight is ice cream and-or bourbon," Linc said as he sat down on the other corner of the table so that their knees were touching.

"Leila, he's a poor bet if that's all he's offering and you're this new into a relationship. Choose me. I would have made sure that hot sex was on the menu, too."

Leila laughed. It felt good. Most of the time she didn't think about it, but there was heavy lifting when it came to Miray Cloud. Her mother could be fierce about some things. But something happening to her husband? Nope. Grant was her rock, and Miray wouldn't be able to cope. Leila would definitely not be able to take any assignments until her dad was up and functional again.

"Sweetheart, what has you thinking so hard?" Linc asked.

"Just know that it isn't about sex with Jase."

"Dammit," Jase whined.

"Do you want to talk about whatever it is?"

"Before I answer that question," she gave Linc a wan smile, "how about if you tell me if I'm right about something?"

"Okay, what?"

"You're already buttering me up with booze and sugar because you're about to deliver bad news, right?"

"It could be bad news, yes."

"Then we'll stick with your topic and put mine away for some other day."

"Fair enough. Booze or sugar?" Linc asked again.

"Neither. I just want to take whatever you've got to tell me straight."

Linc moved his chair a little closer to her so he could put his hand on her thigh. She covered it with hers. Having his heat there on her body helped.

"Everything that happened while you were in Syria, how you were beaten, questioned, and tossed in a hole? That information didn't make its way upward to some of the highest levels of the CIA. Vugar Gadirov is definitely on their watch list, but none of what he has said—or his complex in Syria—were ever updated in his file."

Leila leaned down and propped her head on the table with her free hand. It was exhausting. It was all so exhausting.

"Okay, so Jerry Earnst is a bad guy and keeping all of his report silent. Or they have a spy in the CIA who works for Vugar, which, by the way, the three of us were all pretty sure about, and I told Jerry in my statement."

"Baby, I'm saying your statement never made it into any CIA file."

So tired. Just so damned tired.

"Can't this wait until tomorrow? I'm not processing this real well, and we're talking about something that happened five months ago. This isn't affecting anyone anymore, because somehow the prisoners got released through normal diplomatic channels, and that was the endgame. Game over."

"Kostya and Gideon are coming over tomorrow. Kostya has already been in touch with Caryn Hannover at the CIA; that's how he knows the information hasn't gotten into the system."

Leila pulled her hand out of Linc's clasp, then rubbed

her shoulders with both of her hands. "According to Elijah, this was a top-secret op," she said as she looked from Jase and then back to Linc. "He said only the first assistant director and the director really knew what was going on. Everybody else in the CIA only knew the cover story. If that were true, that would explain why it didn't hit Hannover's desk. It's under her paygrade," she said as she yawned. "There you go, mystery solved. Can I go to bed now?"

"Not quite yet. I want to get you ready for tomorrow's meeting with Kostya, Gideon, and the three of us. I explained to everyone what you said in your witness statement about the attempted kidnapping of your dad. I really think they were attempting to kidnap *you*."

Leila's hands dropped from her neck to the flat of the table. "Are you kidding me?"

Jase wasn't smiling. He looked serious. This was bad.

"But I had to physically hold on to my dad to stop them from taking him. They wanted him."

"Or could it have been they were trying to pull him off of you, so that they could get to you, and take you?"

Bile rose in her throat. "Are you telling me I got my dad almost killed?"

Linc moved his chair then did some fancy SEAL superpower magic, and she found herself sitting on his lap...again. "You did not get your dad almost killed. An operation went south and you're still a target. Hell, Leila, would you have volunteered if you knew what the actual operation was? No."

She wrapped her arms around Linc, wanting to believe everything he was saying, but he was wrong. "Honey, I would have volunteered if Elijah had come clean and told me he was trying to get those people out of a Syrian prison. So, me going to Syria and choosing to work with Elijah is a moot point. I went, even though he didn't tell me everything. Then, if he had told me everything, I would have gone too."

"Leila, it's not your fault," Jase reiterated quietly from across the table.

She pushed herself away from Linc's chest. "Okay, what you're saying sounds plausible. But I've been back from Syria for almost five months. Why wait till now if he wants information from me?"

"I can't answer that unless we have an idea of the information that he wants."

Leila sat up straight. "I know exactly what he wants. I don't know why he wants it. It makes no sense. But the last thing he was asking me before I passed out, he wanted the name of the man in al-Assad's government who would arrange the release."

She saw Linc look over at Jase. "What?" she asked.

"That's it, baby? That's all he wanted?"

Leila nodded. "I couldn't give up the name. The guy was risking his life, and probably all of his family's lives, to help get those prisoners released."

"For five million in diamonds," Jase said with a bit of a sneer.

"I don't care if he was in it for profit or not. He was going to help us rescue those four people. Elijah told me he'd known the guy for over thirty years."

"So, the Director, the First Assistant Director, Elijah, and you know this guy's name. At least we can now say that the Vugar's spy in the CIA isn't either of those two guys because they could have just given him the information and he wouldn't have had to come after you."

She was so tired, and trying to go through all the

mental calculations with him right now was tough, but Leila kept at it.

"That's not true. This guy was Elijah's friend. He never told anybody at Langley who his contact was."

"Fuck," Jase breathed.

"Fuck is right. So, we're stuck with the fact that anybody at the CIA could be our spy. Leila is the only one who has the information that Vugar wants, and he'll stop at nothing to get it."

"Then they'll try to hurt Mom or Dad to get to me," Leila whispered.

Linc jostled her while he got out his phone. He dialed a number and then he put the phone on speaker.

"You got something?"

"Kostya, Leila's listening in. It's me and Jase. We figured out what Vugar wanted from Leila. The info came from Elijah and was never shared with anyone in the CIA, that's why Vugar's spy hasn't been able to supply him with the info."

"What is it?" Kostya bit out the question.

Leila leaned forward over the table so she could be heard better by the phone. "Hi, this is Leila."

"Hi, Leila. I'm so sorry about your dad. How is he doing?" Kostya's tone had immediately changed to someone who was sympathetic and caring. She could see why Linc enjoyed working for him so much.

"Eventually, he should be fine. He won't be running any marathons, but he'll be back to golf, so all is good."

Linc squeezed her waist and winked. He got the fact that she was just trying to stay upbeat.

"Anyway, Lieutenant, I know what Vugar wants."

"Call me Kostya. What does he want?"

"He wants to know the name of the contact in al-

Assad's government who was going to arrange the prisoner release. I can't figure out why that would be of any use to him, but it's what he wanted me to tell him. I couldn't. I was afraid it would blow the release of the prisoners and put a target on his back. He's been a friend of Elijah's for years. I couldn't do it." Leila sucked air between her teeth, remembering that encounter with Vugar.

"Here's why I'm calling," Linc jumped in. "Before a call with Caryn tomorrow, we've got to work out getting Leila's parents to a safehouse, or something. Vugar will definitely use them as leverage to get Leila to talk."

"Agreed," Kostya said. "Gideon and I will still be up there bright and early. I think that Max Hogan might have some juice in the FBI, I'll give him a call too."

"Who is Max Hogan?" Leila asked.

"He's the lieutenant of another Virginia based SEAL team," Kostya explained. "So, I'll call him before we all talk again tomorrow morning."

"Thanks. Talk to you tomorrow," Leila said in the most upbeat voice she could give. Which was nothing. She sounded like she'd run a marathon.

When the call was disconnected, Leila dropped her head on Linc's chest.

"I can't help but feel this is all my fault," she said in a soft voice.

He cuddled her closer. "It's not. You're a victim, the same as your parents. Now, let's go to bed. We can worry about this tomorrow. Okay?"

He tipped her chin up and gave her a tender kiss.

"Okay?" he asked again.

"Okay."

21

YESTERDAY, SHE FELT LIKE SHE WAS SLEEPWALKING. BY NOON the next day, she felt like she was in some crazy fast-forward video.

"Leila, you need to come with us," her mother said again.

"No, *anne*, it's important that you and dad have time alone so that you can take care of him and he can recover. You know he does best when he can see you."

Miray Cloud nodded. "This is true."

Leila looked around and saw Paul Fullerton talking on his mobile phone as he came over to where she was standing next to her mother.

"Miray, it's time to go," he said gently. "Grant's been helicoptered to the secure private hospital upstate. Now we need to get you there with him."

"Shouldn't Leila come?" her mother said for probably the twentieth time.

Paul glanced over Miray's head at Leila and Linc. Leila gave a slight shake of her head, and Paul nodded.

"No, right now it's best to keep her with Linc, who will

manage her safety. Trust me, it's all under control." He went to take Miray's elbow and escort her to one of the three SUVs.

"Hold on, I need another hug," Leila said. She forced back tears as she gave her petite mother a fierce hug. "You keep dad on the straight and narrow, you got that?"

"Of course. I love you, *Bebek*."

"I love you too."

She watched as Paul helped her mother into the backseat and then got in beside her. As soon as they started driving down the road, she felt like a boulder had been lifted off of her shoulders. She turned to Linc.

"Okay, let's go catch this motherfucker."

Linc laughed. "I like your attitude. Jase is locking up your parents' house. Gideon has arranged for us to be staying at another home while all of this shit is being sorted out."

"Hence the need for me to pack," Leila said, nodding at his truck where her suitcases were stored.

"Yes. Gideon and Kostya are already there. We're going to have a strategy session. Gideon says he has even more information."

"Is he just like a slot machine that always pays out?"

Jase laughed as he came up beside them. "You're talking about Gideon, aren't you?"

Leila nodded.

"Leila, you don't know the half of it." Jase grinned.

LINC WAS SURPRISED to see Kostya smiling when he opened the door to the two-story colonial in Columbia, Maryland. "Leila, it's good to see you again."

She smiled at him. "It's good to see you, too. How's Lark doing?"

Kostya's smile got bigger. "She's at the cranky stage. She's having to do more research on articles at home. More phone time, instead of gallivanting all around the world. *I'm* thrilled. Her? Not too much."

Kostya ushered them into the formal living room.

"We're set up in the study. It's big enough to act as a conference room for all of us. Your rooms are upstairs. You can unpack later."

"Can I bring my laptop?" Leila asked.

"What for?" Kostya wanted to know.

"I've been trying to put some scenarios together. I want to share them."

"Then definitely."

They followed him to the back of the house where there was a spacious home office. Gideon was sitting behind one of the two desks. He was on the phone and he had a laptop open in front of him, as well as a tablet lit up on the desk.

"Thanks, Riley. This is exactly what I needed," Gideon said, finishing his call.

He looked up and smiled. Apparently, there was good news. He stood up and rounded the desk to give Leila a hug. "How's your dad?"

"Mom will give me an update when she's at the private hospital and has spent a little time with him."

"That's good."

"Okay, let's sit down. Leila, why don't you set up at the other desk," Kostya suggested. He turned to Gideon. "She has some theories she wants to run by us."

"Good. In the meantime, I'll let you know what I've found out. I can't name methods and sources, but this isn't coming from the CIA, so I'm sure the data is accurate. I actually talked to the person who found this out."

Linc relaxed. That meant it was most likely another SEAL team member. This was good. Very, very good.

"Vugar's name has come up in Somalia. He is a regular supplier of arms to the Al-Shabaab in Somalia, and he's missed delivering on the last three shipments. This is a first for him. He's been the most reliable arms dealer in Africa for the past seven years."

"Okay, so Vugar is screwing up. How recent?" Jase asked.

"The latest intel is he missed a shipment two weeks ago. Now, this next part has not been substantiated. It is rumor only. But Vugar has a younger brother, and he's been Vugar's right hand since he started. He went missing five months ago. Nobody's seen hide nor hair of him. The rumor is that Vugar killed him."

Linc winced. "Killed him, or had him killed?"

"Killed him," Kostya interjected. He said it softly, knowing about Linc's childhood. Linc gave a brief shake of his head, indicating he was fine.

"I've been trying to track down if this is true or not," Gideon said.

"Okay, he killed his brother, and he's failing to meet his commitments. How does that tie into Syria?" Leila asked.

"This is my other piece of firm info. Again, I can't go into methods and sources, but—"

"Would it be better if I left so you could talk more freely?" Leila asked. "I could rustle up lunch," she offered.

"No, it's irrelevant where I got the information, just that it is golden. My source found out where on the dark web that Vugar does most of his business, the buying and selling of arms. He uses one of the ugliest private sites around. He'll put up what he has for sale for forty-eight hours, then people shop, and he's done. Five months ago, about the time Vugar's brother went missing, Vugar was saying he had two Russian nukes for sale. Within five hours, all mention of that was taken down."

"Then how did your source find out about it?" Linc asked.

"My friend has spiders out on the dark web crawling for certain words. When they pop up, he goes in and looks. He's always felt that the CIA was doing the same thing, so there wasn't any reason for him to report it. But he did a screen capture, just for his personal files."

"I like your source," Leila grinned. "I see where you're going with this."

"I don't." Linc said.

"Neither do I," said Jase.

"I forgot you worked as an analyst at the CIA." Gideon smiled. "Solving puzzles was part of your job."

Leila nodded. "But this is a lot of conjecture."

"We're definitely going to need to test our hypothesis. But it's the only thing that sounds reasonable for why Vugar waited five months to make another go at you," Gideon said.

She turned to Linc and Jase.

"Here is a possibility. It kind of makes sense, and I'll have to go to Elijah's friend in Syria, the source, to find out if it's true or not."

"Okay, but what is the possibility?" Linc asked.

"Suppose, besides promising to get people out of prison, this guy also knows how to put his hands on a nuke? It's the only thing that makes sense, because Vugar went after Americans for this information. That's big.

That really puts a target on his back. Hell, Navy SEALs could get mad at him." Leila smiled.

"There's a flaw in your theory right from the start. This guy had to have contacted Vugar to tell him about the nuke, so Vugar doesn't need to ask you for the contact info." Linc sighed. He'd been hoping this would be the answer.

"Let me continue. This is where the right-hand man, the brother comes in. I'm thinking the Syrian went to the little brother. Little brother gets a buyer and takes some money. Vugar finds out and kills him."

"Okay. That's why Vugar doesn't have the contact info and needs you. But sweetheart, here's another fly in the ointment. Why wait for another five months to make a go at you?"

"I think the buyer shows up and is demanding his nuke. I'm thinking Vugar didn't know his brother had basically sold a promise, and now Vugar is stuck holding the bag."

Linc pinched his bottom lip. "You are taking a lot of leaps here."

"You're right, she is," Kostya agreed. "Gideon, is this where you were headed?"

"Yep. Only I was thinking instead of little brother having sold the nuke, and Vugar has to cough it up. Because I don't think any buyer would have waited that long. I'm thinking that somebody out there knew about the post on Vugar's site, and is squeezing him to produce the nuke so he can buy it. Maybe someone bigger and badder than Vugar. Either way, he's fucked."

"We've got to find out if this guy has the nuke. Otherwise, this theory doesn't hold water," Kostya said. "What's his name, and how do you get a hold of him?"

Leila looked over at Linc. He could see how conflicted she was, but he gave her a nod of reassurance.

"His name is Shaker Jassim. He works in al-Assad's presidential palace. I have an encrypted email, where I can put in potential dates and times to meet. Then he'll choose one and tell me where to meet on one of the times I had provided. Elijah must have told him to expect me, because he was worried about the op going south. I'm going to have to go in person."

"You might not. Not if we can use you. I've got friends in the states who can break into almost any computer system. We should be able to at least find all mentions of Shaker Jassim and his friends, family and known associates. Once we have the data, it'll be thrown into an AI translator, and we should be able to tell if he really has anyone who could get him information on a nuclear weapon."

"God yes, do that," Linc said. "Leila isn't going over to Syria again."

"If I need to go, I'll go," Leila stated as she turned on Linc. "I will finish what was started. Are we clear?"

"Fine. You'll go with a bunch of friends of mine who'll be taking some personal time off to visit Damascus with you." Linc had found his happy, and she was named Leila, and he'd be damned if he would let anything happen to her.

22

"Leila and I are going for a walk," Linc said as soon as he threw his and Leila's plates into the dishwasher. None of the other three men looked surprised, only Leila did.

"Let me change shoes," she said.

"You doing okay?" Jase asked as he moved to the kitchen and rinsed off his dinner plate as well.

"Nope. I don't like it when international terrorists are focused on my woman."

Jase put his hand on Linc's shoulder and squeezed. "We'll protect her, you know that."

Linc nodded.

"I'm ready," Leila said as she came down the stairs.

Linc opened the door for her, then followed and grabbed her hand when they got to the sidewalk.

Leila sighed. "You're armed. Why does Jase need to follow us?"

"It's just part of the service." Linc put his arm around her shoulders and tucked her in close to his body.

"So, what did you want to talk about?" Leila asked.

"That's my line. Your life has been taken over by me and my team for the last couple of days. I figure you might want to talk about some things."

Leila wrapped her arm around his waist so that they could be even closer. "Yeah, I do have something to say. This is a biggie. You can't tell me what I can or cannot do. That's a deal-breaker for me. You and I can discuss things, but I will not be dictated to just because we are together."

Linc swallowed. *Fuck.* He'd fucked up. Big time. He could hear it in her voice. And now she was hitting him on something that he wasn't sure he could fix.

"Leila, I'm in this relationship one hundred percent. I have never been in love before, and I intend for us to go the distance. Please, baby, please know that I will do my damndest never to dictate to you, but where your safety is concerned my gut is to protect the women I love. It's a knee-jerk reaction."

She said nothing as they walked for another five minutes.

"Linc, I think you just said you loved me," she whispered.

He gave a relieved chuckle. She wasn't kicking him to the curb. "Yes, I did. Why are you whispering?"

"Because if I'm dreaming, I don't want to wake up."

Linc wanted to kiss her, but he couldn't. He needed to stay hyper-aware of their surroundings. They needed to get back to the house before he could kiss her.

"I love you, too," she whispered.

Her words hit him in the gut. He felt unadulterated joy. He'd felt the same way the day he got his Trident pin and became a Navy SEAL, and that day when he was ten years old and he could legally take George Hart's last name.

"Let's get back to the house," he whispered.

LEILA WOKE up to the sound of herself screaming as she was struggling to get away from someone.

"It's okay, I've got you. It's me, Lincoln. I've got you, baby."

He held her so her face was buried in his neck. "Smell me, baby, you're safe."

Every time she woke up screaming, he would hug her, and then pull her close and tell her to breathe in his scent. Insist she smell him. And every time, it worked. She immediately calmed and felt safe.

"Linc," she said as she tried to understand where she was.

"Linc," she said again, finally melting into his embrace.

"Yes, Beauty, it's me. Was it the same dream?"

It took a moment for her to collect her thoughts. Linc didn't push, he just kind of rocked her. Safe. She felt safe.

"The dream was all over the place. Sometimes it's Katherine bleeding on top of me. Sometimes it's my mom in the well. This time it was my dad instead of Elijah who was dragged away by the terrorists."

"That's heavy-duty stuff."

"It'll pass." At least she prayed it would.

"I'm sorry that I wake up everybody in the house."

"It just gives everybody a chance to take a piss. It's all good."

Leila laughed a little, which she knew was Linc's hope. He tucked her back under the covers and pulled her down so her head was resting on his chest.

"When this settles, you're going to see someone, aren't you?"

Leila gave another small laugh.

"That was tough for you, wasn't it? Asking instead of telling."

Linc cupped the back of her head. "Yes, it was. I just want to take care of the women in my life. I learned early on that life can be ugly. I'll always want to protect you from the ugly and make sure you're safe."

Leila heard the hurt in his voice. "It sounds like you have a hot button that is as bad as mine where I don't like being told what to do. Asked is fine. Told, not so much."

"I'm going to do my best not to dictate to you," Linc promised.

"Maybe if I knew why you are so intent on keeping me safe and protected, I could handle it better when you end up trying to tell me what to do. Can you do that?"

She felt his heart rate increase and knew that whatever he was going to say would be bad.

"What's your first memory as a kid?" Linc asked her.

"Easy. I was on top of a horse with my dad. I felt like I was as high as the sky. I love horses to this day."

"That's a wonderful memory." Linc placed a kiss on the top of her head. "My very first memory was mom lying in the upstairs hallway, crying. My dad was towering over her, yelling something, then he picked her up by the scruff of her neck and hit her in the stomach and she dropped to the floor again. When he pounded his feet down to his bedroom, I sneaked down the hall to see what was wrong with her. When I tried to wake her up, she told me she was resting, and I needed to go back to my room."

"I spent the first six years of my life going to my room, as my dad used my mom as a punching bag."

Linc paused, and Leila looked up at him through her lashes. She could see he was thinking, and it didn't look like he was done with the story.

"Another memory was when I was in school. There was a policeman who talked to our class who told us they were there to help us. If there was something that our moms or dads couldn't help us with, and somebody was in danger, we should call 911. I remember that school day really well."

Again, he paused.

Leila prayed she wasn't tensing up. If he felt she was afraid he'd stop talking. She did her best just to continue with the languid circles on his chest. Instead of a kiss, she licked his nipple. He gave her a quick squeeze.

"The next time I heard my mom scream and moan for my dad to stop, I snuck down to the kitchen and stepped up onto a chair to get to the phone on the wall. I called 911. I was scared shitless. I knew if he saw me he might even whale on me for the first time, and he'd hit Mom even worse. I remember thinking that if I called 911, that same cop from school would show up."

This time, Leila didn't care if she was obvious, if he felt her empathy. She wrapped her arm around him and pulled him closer. He cupped her ass and arranged it so that their bodies pressed together in the way they liked.

He still said nothing more.

"Did the police arrive?" she finally asked.

"Yeah. I opened my bedroom window and listened to my dad lie to one cop, and then I listened to my mom swear my dad had never abused her. He was smart, that fucking bastard. He aimed for the stomach, sides, thighs. Places that didn't leave marks that people might notice. Since she would not press charges, they left."

Leila felt herself tense up. She knew the story was going to get worse. For what seemed like an eternity, but was actually only two to three minutes, Linc said nothing.

"Linc?"

He gave a heavy sigh. "After the cops were gone, he marched into my bedroom, yelling that he knew I'd called the cops. To this day, I can't understand the psyche of a man who would beat on women and children. But there he was, whaling away on me and when my mom tries to stop him, he hits her so hard she lands against the wall."

Linc took a deep breath. He looked down at Leila and saw a tear on her cheek. He brushed it away with his thumb. "We're in the homestretch, baby. You ready for the end?"

Leila nodded.

"While my dad is beating me with one of his belts, my mom must have got the pistol that was in the house, because he stops beating me. He gets up, and I roll to the floor. He's telling her not to do it. And then I hear a roar, and I pass out."

"Good for her."

"You realize she killed him, right?"

"I hope he was gut shot and took forever to bleed out."

A hoarse laugh was ripped from Linc's soul.

"Was she charged?" Leila asked.

"Nope. They said it was in self-defense."

"I'm surprised you didn't want to become a cop when you grew up."

"No, that wasn't going to happen. I didn't want to swallow vomit when I had to go out on domestic disturbance calls and have the woman tell me she wasn't being beaten. I went for special forces because the enemy was clearly labeled, and my job was to take down the enemy."

"When you've talked about your mother and stepfather and your brothers and sisters, it sounds like you have a great family."

"I do have a great family. My mom busted her ass to make sure that she pulled herself out of the mindset that it was okay to be beaten. She made sure that both of us got into counseling. That's why I'm recommending it so strongly to you. I didn't really know what was happening as a kid. But we had long talks about it when I was a teenager. My mom is a survivor, just like you."

"My mom is going to love you," Linc said. Leila shivered as he stroked his hand under her sleep shirt, and started stroking her up and down. "Now I think it's time for us to go back to sleep."

Leila let her hand drift down from his chest until she reached his bellybutton, then she circled that. She pulled back the covers and got up on her knees.

"Lincoln Hart, I don't think it's going to be possible for you to go to sleep with this big problem in your way. I've got just the thing that will help."

Linc let himself be coaxed out of his boxers. Leila loved the look of his cock. She circled it with her hand near the crown, then slid downward to the root, where she couldn't circle it because it was too thick. Linc arched upward and there was a bit of pre-come on the top of his cock.

Yummy.

Leila bent over him and took him deeply into her mouth, humming with pleasure. This was wonderful. The taste, scent, and feel of him overwhelmed her.

"You've got such a hot mouth, baby. I love the way you

can take all of me," he said as he slipped his fingers through her hair. He knew never to pull after she'd told him more details about how Vugar handled her.

She violently shut that door in her mind and focused on Linc instead.

Her tongue paid special attention to his sweet spot. As she would slowly release his penis from her mouth, she used the tip of her tongue under the crown of his cock and swirled, licked, and teased. Again, she took him deep into her mouth, even deeper, breathing through her nose as she gradually pulled upwards until she released him with a pop.

"Leila," he groaned.

She loved the way he smelled and tasted. Clean, masculine, Linc. When she felt his big hand palm her head, just touching her, she relaxed even more into the beautiful pleasure of sucking his cock. Every groan or hiss that came out of his mouth was like music.

His thumb brushed against her forehead, pushing up.

"I'm going to come," he whispered.

She couldn't wait. She smiled around his erection and did another slide downward, while her right hand caressed his testicles, and he let out a loud groan.

It was a good one.

"Stop, baby, I want in your pussy."

He would not get what he wanted. She wanted to make him come this way. On the next downward stroke, Leila ran the tip of her fingernail from the root of his cock, over his scrotum, to his anus.

Linc shuddered and moaned her name as she milked every drop he had to give her, then she swallowed it down. She slowly slid her mouth upward, and once again released his cock with a popping noise. Then she kissed the tip for good measure.

She leaned back on her knees and looked down at his glittering eyes.

This man was a treasure that she intended to keep.

23

Linc spent a while just looking at Leila in the morning light. She truly was beautiful. Inside and out. She scared him, though. She wasn't in the military, but she had the heart of a warrior, and was willing to do whatever was necessary to help save the world. He was going to do his best to not tell her what to do, but he was going to get very good at the art of debating.

He slid out of bed and put the covers back up around her. He needed coffee and to see what was going on before he took a shower. He threw on his camo pants and a t-shirt and went downstairs to see who was up.

Gideon was standing beside the coffeemaker with his mug under the spout.

"I think you're supposed to put the carafe on the burner, not your mug." Linc smiled as he grabbed a banana from out of the fruit bowl and enjoyed Gideon scowling at him. When Gideon's mug was full, he made a quick switch with the carafe without wasting a drop of coffee. Then Linc watched as Gideon went to the freezer and pulled out an ice cube. He dropped it in his mug of coffee and eyed Linc.

"You weren't kidding about those nightmares."

"No. I wasn't."

"Has she been like that ever since Syria?"

Linc shook his head, chewing on his banana. He swallowed. "Maybe four or five since we've been sleeping together, but nothing like this. She remembered a lot of her nightmare last night. She told me about it. She was mixing up her dad getting shot with images of her time in Syria. She still hasn't gone to counseling, but she promises to now."

Gideon took a sip of his coffee and smiled. Linc threw away the banana peel, then poured himself a cup of coffee.

"A lot of information came in last night. The most notable is Leila's friend, Shaker has a pretty well-connected wife. She's Russian, and three of her brothers are in the Russian mob, and her father is retired Russian military. Before he retired, he oversaw the dismantling of Russian atomic weapons, in accordance with the International Atomic Energy Agency guidelines."

"How come al-Assad isn't using the wife to get his hands on things?" Linc asked. "She's a ripe target."

"She came over to Syria with her baby sister when she was eleven to live with relatives. I'm guessing that her mother probably saw how the brothers were turning out and wanted a better life for her daughters. So, she changed her name to El Din, and assimilated into Syrian society. Maybe a little too well, because now she, her children, and her husband are too high profile to leave without a big bankroll."

"So, he's our guy," Linc said, drinking his coffee. "It is a nuclear weapon."

"Actually, it's two," Gideon corrected.

"Even better," Linc said sarcastically. He went over to the cupboard and got down another mug. He poured some coffee, creamer, and sugar into it. "Taking this up to Leila, and we'll get this party started. But Caryn Hanover is out of the picture now, right?"

Gideon nodded. "Yep, she will not be any part of this."

"Good."

Linc set her mug of coffee on the nightstand, then kissed her forehead. "Time to get up," he whispered in her ear.

"Don't wanna."

"I have coffee right here, doctored up the way you like it." He picked up the mug and waved it next to her nose. He saw her grin. She pushed up on the bed and propped pillows behind herself so she could sit up more easily.

"What time is it?"

He looked at his watch. "Seven hundred hours."

"You know you're sexy when you do military speak, right?" she asked right before she took a sip of her coffee.

"I didn't know, but glad to hear it."

"I better get moving. Gideon might have some information." She sounded like a kid on Christmas morning.

"He does."

"What is it? Give me. Give me."

"Shaker is probably the guy. His wife has ties to a retired Russian military officer who was in charge of dismantling nuclear weapons."

"So, one or two didn't get dismantled, huh?"

"Sounds like."

"I'm going to call Mom and check on Dad. Then I'm going to grab a shower, and I'll meet you down there."

"I'm making breakfast. What do you want?"

"Surprise me."

She leaned over and reached for her smartphone and pressed in her mom's number. Linc left her to it.

When he got back downstairs, Jase had already found a waffle iron and was mixing up some batter. Linc smelled bacon.

"Where's the bacon?" Linc asked.

"I'm broiling it. That way grease doesn't get all over everything, and it cooks more evenly," Jase said.

Linc nodded. "Gideon? Kostya?"

"They're calling Lark and Jada. Kostya checks in a lot. Have you noticed?"

"Is there something to be worried about with Lark's pregnancy?" Linc asked Jase. "Something they're not telling us?"

"That's not the vibe I'm picking up. I think he worries about her, sure. But I really think he wants her to know he's thinking about her."

"My stepfather is like that. That's the kind of husband I want to be."

Jase poured some batter into the waffle iron. He looked over Linc's shoulder to check out the stairway. "You thinking about marriage with Leila?" Jase asked quietly.

"She doesn't know it yet, but we're destined to grow old together."

Jase smiled. "Kind of like my parents, too."

"That's the plan."

"DON'T you think the PowerPoint presentation for three people is over the top?" Jase asked Gideon.

"Don't mess with his mojo," Leila shushed Jase. "I like a good PowerPoint presentation. Thanks for creating one, Gideon."

Linc enjoyed having Leila sitting by him on the couch in the office. He was thankful that Gideon found a way to project the presentation on the wall. This way he could snuggle with Leila.

"These are the different sites where Russia used to have all of their retired atomic missiles that they had in the queue to dismantle. As of three years ago they haven't let the International Atomic Energy Agency into any of their sites to see if they are being dismantled in accordance to their international treaty."

"This is a shitty time for there to be any nuclear weapons out in the wild. This needs to be stopped." Kostya got up from his chair and actually patted his pants. Linc knew he was looking for a cigarette, but there were none. He had quit smoking years ago. But whenever Kostya looked for a cigarette, you knew he was stressed.

"Seems to me, the selling of the nuclear weapon is higher than any of our paygrades," Gideon said. "And with the state of the world right now, having nuclear weapons stolen from Russia will cause a huge uprising. One finger will point at the other to blame them."

"You're right. During my stint in Russia, that is exactly how certain people think. It would be best for everyone involved if my name didn't come up," Leila said.

"Agreed," Linc said. "But right now, we're not

concentrating on the nuclear weapon, are we?" he asked Kostya and Gideon.

"No," Kostya answered. "We're not. I've already bumped this up to Captain Hale. I would be surprised if he won't be talking to the Chief of Naval Operations today."

"Holy hell, that's definitely high on the food chain," Jase said.

"Okay, so we'll be in charge of stopping Vugar, right?" As soon as Jase opened his mouth, Leila gave him the hand. "I don't need any more smart remarks out of you today, got it?"

He nodded, but Linc could also see he was having trouble not laughing.

"Keep going, Gideon. What else did you find out?" Leila asked.

"Vugar has a mansion in Florida, and his private plane left Germany for Miami a week ago." Gideon pulled a picture of a beautiful home in Florida. Linc noticed a dog near the gate. With dogs, this would be a little tougher to break into than the home in Syria.

"That just lends more credence to the fact that it was Vugar who was behind the kidnapping attempt, and he was out after Leila," Gideon said, pointing out the obvious.

"I'm the only thing that's going to flush Vugar out of hiding, aren't I?" Leila asked the room in general.

"No," Linc said vehemently. "We know where he is. We'll take him out."

"You can't do that," Leila sighed. "You don't have probable cause for a search warrant, and if you did, this would have to be handled by the FBI."

"Leila's right, he's out after her. Somehow, we have to

convince him she's alone and he can take her," Gideon said as he turned off the presentation.

Kostya looked up from his phone. "We have little time to put together a plan to set Leila up as a target, if that's what she wants to do." He looked over at Leila with a compassionate expression. "Somebody went through your family home last night. They tore up the house from top to bottom. All of us agree. They had to be looking for something that would explain where you might be."

"I still want to go over there and get some of my things," she said stubbornly.

"You can't." Linc said. "If you go there, something could happen to you, and I could never live with myself."

"Linc is right; they're going to have that house under surveillance," Kostya explained. "Unless we want that to be where we make our last stand to get Vugar, I suggest you don't go in there, and instead let one of us get whatever you need."

"Won't they see you and try to stop you?"

"There are so many FBI agents milling around your house right now, one of us stopping by won't make a difference," Kostya assured her.

"Leila, what are you planning on getting? You have clothes with you here. You have your laptop. So, what is it you need?"

Linc watched as she bit her lip.

"I wanted to get some of the stuff Dad would like so I could send it to him. It was a stupid idea. There's no need to do that."

Linc laced his fingers through hers and squeezed her hand in support. "It's not a stupid idea. I totally understand. But it's not worth the risk, is it?" he asked.

"No, it isn't," she agreed. "How do we set up a trap for Vugar to kidnap me?" she asked Gideon.

"I see your dad owns some property at the Lake of the Woods, in Virginia. Have you been?" Gideon asked.

"Almost every year of my childhood. I love that place."

"Because your dad inherited it, he rolled the title into your family trust. Therefore, it didn't pop up when I did an initial search for properties owned by you or anyone in your family. But I found it late last night."

"That would be a great place to make a stand," Leila said. "It's easy to defend."

"That's good to know, Leila." Kostya gave her a sharp nod. "Gideon, how do you know they'll find this information if it took you and your team this long to find it?"

"Easy." Gideon smiled. "I'm going to change the name on the title from their LLC as the owner and put down Grant and Miray Cloud. I'm going to do this after we get set up at the cabin."

"I guess we better get moving again," Linc said as he stood up and held out his hand to help her up off the couch.

24

It was dark by the time they started driving up the dirt driveway that led to the summer cabin Leila remembered so well. A dog ran around the side of the house and was at her window, licking the glass when they parked behind the cabin.

"Roscoe, I can't get out, you dufus. You're too heavy. Move back."

The next thing she knew, Linc was out of the stopped vehicle and was over to her side in an instant. With a few muffled words that Leila couldn't understand, he got Roscoe sitting beside him so that he could open the door and let her get out.

Roscoe was doing a full-body shiver. He was so excited to see her.

"He's the neighbor's dog," Leila explained as she went down on her haunches to give him an all-over rub. "I usually have treats for him, but I forgot this time."

He didn't seem to care as he circled her and Linc all the way to the front door and herded them into the cabin. Linc grinned. The dog was a mutt, but he definitely had some collie mixed in there the way he liked to herd his people.

"Why did both Kostya and Gideon need to go pick up Jonas and Mateo from the airport? Hopefully, it was just to give us a little alone time." Leila waggled her eyebrows as Linc put down her bags.

"I expect Kostya is going to be talking to Captain Hale about the nuke, and he didn't feel comfortable doing it someplace where you might hear. Then he and Gideon definitely wanted to discuss strategy."

"And Jase?"

"He was right behind us. Then we lost him."

Linc looked down at his phone. Then he smiled and looked up at her. "He texted me one word. Groceries."

"I can't believe how much that man eats." Leila laughed.

"You should see him when we've really spent the day training, and the number of calories he can take in after that. He'll order two complete meals, then two desserts. He's huge, but there isn't an ounce of fat on the guy."

"So where does Roscoe come from?" Linc asked.

"There's a house about three hundred feet to the right of us. They have their own drive off the main highway, that's why you didn't see them. Anyway, Roscoe belongs to them on paper, but to the rest of the neighborhood in reality. He greets every neighbor as we show up. He's never met someone he doesn't like."

Leila did a onceover of the small living room and dining room area and smiled. It looked just like she remembered. "So, what do you think of the view?" she asked Linc.

Linc came over and put his hand around her waist and

looked down into her face. "I think the view is lovely. How are you doing, Leila?" he asked.

"Actually, I'm doing pretty good, knowing I'll actually be free of this madman soon."

Linc stroked his thumb over her lower lip and she trembled. Just that one touch and she was putty in his hands.

"Wanna go upstairs and claim our bedroom before the others get here?" His voice came out raspy.

"Great idea." She led him up the narrow staircase to one of the three bedrooms on the top floor. "This is the one with a queen bed. Everything else has twin beds."

"You chose well," Linc said as he tugged off her sweater and kissed a long path from her jaw, down her neck to her collarbone, on down to the tips of her fingers. "You're gorgeous."

"We're going to have to hurry. This bed squeaks like crazy, so this is our opportunity to get to business while we're here."

Linc didn't bother to respond. He just herded her to the bed and pushed her to sit down on the side of it. The bed let out a loud squeak when she sat down. He chuckled. Then he bent down and untied her sneakers and took off her socks.

"Lose the tank top, Leila," he commanded. She shivered again. It had been a really warm day, and this spring evening was still warm, but she still shivered uncontrollably as his fingers touched from her skull to her tailbone.

"Lift up," he said as he pulled her jeans and panties off.

When he threw her clothes in a pile behind him, he

lifted higher on his knees and unclipped the back of her bra and threw that behind him as well.

Her nipples thrust out like little spikes of want that were begging for his attention. He sucked one diamond-hard tip into his mouth and savored all the textures of her breast. The softness of her skin that then became this beautiful nipple that was rich with nerve endings he delighted in awakening.

Leila put her hands on his shoulders to steady herself, but that wasn't what he wanted. Not this time. "Keep your hands behind your back, okay?" he asked.

She nodded her acquiescence, and stretched her toned arms behind her back, forcing her breasts into higher prominence. Just for him, only for him. He went back and forth between each breast, licking them, nipping at them, loving them. The sighs and moans of pleasure coming from Leila made him rock hard.

"Touch my clit, Linc."

"First you're going to have to ride me."

LINC UNDID HIS BELT BUCKLE, pulled a condom out of his pocket, then untucked his erection that was begging for release. He sheathed himself in protection, then picked her up and lowered her onto his cock, one slow inch at a time. It felt like he was encased in a hot fist of wet velvet. He looked up from where they were joined and studied the visual feast that was Leila Cloud.

Her rounded stomach undulated as she moved up and down on him, driving him out of his mind. Then, as he looked up farther, there was the gentle sway of her full breasts, as his thrusts got a little harder. And her face.

That half-lidded look of wonder and lust made him so much harder.

He grabbed her around the waist and pulled her down as he thrust upwards. Now her tits began to jiggle.

"Play with your nipples, Leila," he commanded.

Big brown eyes looked up at him. "You promised to touch my clit. To rub me. To make me come."

"And I will. But first you have to show me how you like your breasts played with."

"So, I get to move my hands now?" she teased.

"Do you want to come, or don't you?" he asked hoarsely.

She lifted her hands and encompassed each breast. Then she squeezed them softly, over and over again. When she let go, they seemed even more swollen. He watched, fascinated, as she brought one of her thumbs to her lips and sucked it deep inside her mouth. Then she let go of it with a pop. It was wet.

She took her time to bring her other thumb to her mouth and slowly circle it with her puffy lips, then release it so that it glistened in the lamplight. She took her two wet thumbs and traced circles around her nipples, making them even harder. Again and again, she did that until she took each tip between her thumb and forefinger and pinched and let out a long moan. He groaned.

Linc shoved her hand away from her right breast and sucked her deep into his mouth, somehow keeping up the rhythm that he knew was driving them both mad. He suckled and teased her breast as he pushed his thumb into her mouth.

He watched as she looked even more turned on as she sucked his thumb deep, swirling her tongue around it repeatedly, like she had his dick the night before. He yanked his thumb out of her mouth before he lost all control. He needed to make her come first.

He pressed her swollen clit with his slick thumb, then circled her. Her moans of pleasure became louder the harder he pressed. His other hand went around and clutched her ass, and he pistoned deeper.

"Linc, I'm going to come."

He chuckled. "That's the idea," he said through gritted teeth.

"Come with me," she begged as she did that little twist-undulation thing as she came back down on his cock.

He pinched her clit, and she gasped his name. He didn't know how she did it, because he didn't have any power left as he released himself inside the woman he loved.

TEN MINUTES LATER, they made their way downstairs and found Jase cooking. "Did you know the walls are paper thin around here?" he asked casually.

Linc grinned, but Leila blushed and looked uncomfortable.

"Don't be an asshole. Now you've upset Leila."

Jase looked at Leila. "I'm sorry, honey. The walls aren't paper thin."

"Yes, they are. I remember from when I used to come here as a kid."

"Well, luckily you both are quiet lovers," Jase said as he diced up a tomato.

Leila laughed. "You're so full of shit."

She watched as Jase cut a square of cheese off the

brick and whistled. Roscoe perked up, then Jase threw him the square and Roscoe caught it in his mouth and began to happily munch.

"Cool dog. Who does he belong to?" Jase asked.

"The neighbors to the right, but actually this whole little community. Off this driveway are five houses. We kind of stick together and help one another out if we're around."

"Nice."

All three of their heads popped up when they heard another vehicle come down the private driveway.

"That can't be them. Their ETA is still another hour, isn't it?" Jase asked as he looked at Linc.

"It's somebody who is lost. It happens all the time. I'll go out and give him directions."

She saw Linc's scowl. "Of course, I'll be taking you, Honey Lumpkins. A girl like me can't possibly talk to a stranger in the dark without getting killed."

She went back to the chair where she had taken off her shoes and put them on with her new outfit of jeans and a big flannel shirt.

"I'm ready, H.L."

"H.L.?" Linc asked as he met her at the door.

"Honey Lumpkins of course."

Linc chuckled.

They walked over together to the blue truck. It was just one man in the driver's seat. One hand rested against his steering wheel, one hanging outside the window.

"How are you doing, sir? Can I help you?" Leila asked.

"I think I'm lost. I went down another one of these roads, but nobody would come out of their house to help me. I figured if I just stayed in my truck where you could see my hands, someone would help."

Leila smiled. "Who are you looking for?" she asked.

"I'm looking for Number Four, Angler Way."

She'd never seen or heard of a Street called Angler Way. Something was up.

Leila bit her lower lip. "I'm not all that good with addresses unless I've been to that house. But if you tell me their name, I'll be able to tell you where to go."

"Rogers. Buddy Rogers."

"I'm sorry, I can't help you. But if you go back out the way you came and stop at the gas station right before you turn onto the highway, you'll get good cell reception and you can call your friend."

"Thanks, that's a great idea." The man waved.

As soon as the truck drove off, she turned to Linc. "There's no such street called Angler Way. That guy was lying."

He grabbed her hand and they started running to the house.

"So, I'm making tacos. Not just any old tacos. These are the famous Drakos family tacos," Jase called out as they came back in the front door.

"Jase. Go to your car and bring in all the firepower you can. We've just been cased."

Leila watched as Jase turned off the heat on the burners and covered the seasoned taco meat. She tried to take in Linc's words.

Then, without a word, he raced to his car and opened his trunk and pulled out a full duffle bag. She could see Linc doing something similar with his truck.

"Leila, pull out anything you think you can work with in close quarters, and also what you can handle further away," Jase said. He was serious for once.

"I want a Sig Sauer and a couple of knives for me. I'd like another small gun that I can hide with me."

Jace put the Sig into her hands and Linc lifted her jeans pant leg and attached a knife sheath and a deadly looking knife. "I think you need a shoulder holster for the pistol and a sheath that you can attach to your belt."

She heard Kostya's voice on Linc's phone speaker.

"How sure are you that you were cased?" Kostya asked. Linc described the situation, and Kostya agreed. "Plus, he spotted Leila."

"How far, Gideon?" Kostya asked.

"If we can avoid this traffic ahead, maybe another half hour? I'll see what we can do to cut the time down," Gideon promised.

"Linc, I want updates," Kostya said.

"You got it," Linc replied. Then hung up. He turned his attention to Jase and Leila. He and Jase had worked together for years. They had a rhythm. He was good at going places and not being seen. He could track. He was going to be on the ground. Linc was going to be up high.

"There's only one way in by car, which is the driveway. But there are multiple points of entry through the woods on either side of the cabin. I'm going to take to the roof and take my shots when I can get them."

"I'm going to head to the woods," Jase said.

"Why don't we just drive away?" Leila asked reasonably.

"The blue truck will block off our escape route," Linc said.

"Okay," Leila said.

"I want you inside the house, in the bedroom facing the lake. Get in front of the window facing the east. You'll be able to pick off anybody who gets by me. Jase, you take the west side of the woods. Leila, I want you to take Roscoe into the bedroom with you. Somebody will think twice before entering the bedroom if they hear a dog barking."

He saw the fear behind Leila's resolution. Goddammit, this was the same woman who was just screaming in the middle of the night because of her nightmares, and now this. How much more was she going to have to put up with?

He pulled her into his arms and gave her a fierce kiss.

"I love you. You can do this, baby."

"I love you too. Stay safe."

25

LINC GOT ON THE ROOF AND RELIED ON JASE TO EXPLAIN TO Leila how to handle the night vision goggles. He would just rely on his rifle's night vision scope. Jase and he had their normal communication system. She would have to use her phone. At least they had an extra set of body armor though it was huge on her. But they had to work with what they had.

He called Leila.

"Yeah?" she answered.

"Keep this line open. Keep it on mute unless you have info. Whisper. I'll do the same."

"Got it."

He settled in, keeping his rifle moving slowly so that he could cover both sides of the driveway. He waited. It took eight minutes before anyone had anything to say.

He was the one to break the silence.

Linc picked up his phone and also whispered in his mic, "Incoming. Just one. Twelve-hundred meters out. I'm waiting."

The man was wearing night vision goggles. The longer

Linc could hold off shooting him, the better. He didn't want to alert these people of his presence and he wanted to take out as many targets as he could as fast as he could, when he started shooting.

Linc counted. He was at thirty-three when he heard Jase. "One down."

Nice.

"Did you tell Leila to wait until they were closer before she should shoot?" Linc whispered into his mic really quietly so Leila wouldn't hear.

"Dude, she knows the range of her pistol. She's got it covered." Linc could barely hear what Jase said, but he did. He should have known Leila would have it covered.

Linc waited some more, then he saw another target coming on the other side of the driveway, still about eight hundred meters out. They were moving slowly. Cautiously. Normally, this would be smart on their part, but they didn't know they had a sniper on them.

"One is in range of the house," Leila said.

"Jase?" Linc asked.

"I've got my eye on two."

"On my mark."

"Three. Two. Fire."

Linc only heard five shots. There was momentary silence, then he heard the sound of an automatic rifle.

"Who's being fired on?" Linc demanded to know.

"Not me," Leila answered.

"Not me, either," Jase answered. "It's coming from the east woods. I'm heading that way."

Linc grimaced as he moved to the north side of the roof so he could provide cover for his teammate.

Jase went in with his automatic rifle, lighting up the night.

Linc spotted the source of the return fire. He took careful aim and shot. The rifle fire continued.

He'd missed.

Jase was almost to the east woods and Linc didn't want him in there. He took five more rapid shots in a tight circle. The rifle fire sputtered out. Jase ran into the woods.

"You got him," Jase told Linc.

"I'm going for the guy in the truck," Linc said as he shimmied off the roof. "Jase, you check in with Leila."

"Already on my way."

Linc took to the side of the road, staying in the shadows. He really hadn't expected to see the truck, but there it was. He was on the phone, speaking in Arabic. He was sweating bullets. Linc needed to take this guy alive. He would be their way to finding Vugar.

He pulled out his Sig Sauer and crept up behind him. Linc understood three words. *Sir. Sorry. Death.* Yeah, this guy was talking to Vugar, and he was a dead man walking. Their team needed him. Jase needed to question him.

"I've got the guy from the truck. He's alive for questioning. We can use him to find Vugar," Linc said into his mic.

When he got close enough, he hit him on the side of the head with the butt of his gun. Hard enough so that he'd go down, but soft enough that he wouldn't be unconscious for long. Linc used zip ties on his hands and feet, then threw him in the bed of the truck and drove up to the house.

"Just got the word from Gideon," Jase said as Linc hopped out of the truck. "He's five minutes away. He's bummed he missed all the fun."

LEILA TRIED to be polite to the new men—Jonas Wulff and Mateo Aranda—but she was bone-tired and just wanted to sleep for twenty-four hours. Linc was staying close by, which was great, because she didn't think she could manage if he wasn't.

She'd been so scared that Jase or Linc would die, and the fact that they still hadn't captured Vugar made her stomach turn.

Kostya came out to the back porch where she and Linc were sitting.

"I've got some good news."

Leila lifted her head off of Linc's shoulder. "Yeah?"

"Jase has gotten this guy to talk. He wants an American prison instead of being out in the cold where Vugar can get to him. He actually met up with Vugar yesterday in Washington DC, so that's good news. Means he's nearby. We can get a lock on this guy, take him down, and hand him over to DHS."

Leila perked up. "I like that. With his ties to the CIA, he probably would have escaped, but Homeland Security will know what to do with him."

"Exactly," Kostya smiled.

Jase opened the door. "Is this a private party or can anyone join?" he asked.

Roscoe followed him outside and put his head on Leila's knee.

"You did good work, Jase," Kostya complimented.

Leila watched Jase carefully, and she could see that the compliment meant a lot to him.

"Well, all of you come inside. I rescued the tacos, so let's eat something before DHS agents descend."

"It's after midnight," Leila protested.

"Aren't you hungry?" Jase asked reasonably.

Leila thought about it and realized she was.

"Let me take Roscoe home first. Then I can eat. Okay?"

Jase gave her a warm smile. "I'll make sure there's stuff left for you."

"I'm going with her. Are you going to save some for me?" Linc asked.

"Nope. I don't like you as much."

Kostya and Leila laughed.

When Leila got up off the porch swing and started walking, Roscoe immediately followed. Linc put his arm around her and they walked along the lakeshore together.

"Leila?"

"Hmm."

"How is your dad doing?"

"I talked to him on the phone today, which was the first time. I've been so scared, Linc."

"I know."

She loved it when he squeezed her tighter.

"Do you know how much I love you?" Linc asked.

"I've been catching on." She smiled. "I love you, too."

She saw the Murphys' house and Roscoe ran up to the sliding glass door, which was closed. *Poor baby, he couldn't get in.* Usually they left it cracked for him.

"I was wondering, how married are you to living in DC?"

Leila felt her heart beat so fast, she thought it would come out of her chest. "I'm a free agent. It doesn't matter where I live. Why?" she asked breathlessly.

He stopped her in her tracks and stepped in front of her so that all she could see was him. "I want you to relocate to Little Creek and move in with me."

"You do?"

"Absolutely. I can't stand being apart from you. I want

your things in my home, and want your crap on my bathroom sink, I love you."

Leila didn't think about her answer; her heart started talking first. "Yes!"

"Thank God."

She flung her arms around his neck. And pressed kisses all along his jaw and neck until he bent down and she could kiss his lips.

Roscoe bounded back to them. He definitely wanted to be next to the happy people.

Leila was shaking. She was so happy.

Linc pushed the hair off her face and gave her a tender kiss. "We are definitely not staying in the room with the creaky bed tonight. I'm finding us a hotel."

She grinned.

Roscoe jumped up on them.

"He really wants in on the action." Leila grinned as she bent down and rubbed him all over. He bounded up to his house and pushed at the closed sliding glass door, then he whined.

The door opened, and Roscoe bounded inside. Then he let out a sharp yelp before going silent.

Leila ran up to the door, wanting to know what was wrong.

"Stop," Linc yelled.

Leila got to the door just a hair faster than Linc, who stayed behind her.

Inside, she saw Mr. and Mrs. Murphy duct-taped to their dining room chairs.

"This is so convenient," Vugar said as Leila stared at the scared eyes of her neighbors above their duct-taped mouths. "I thought I was going to have to call you to come over, but instead you come to me, like some sort of present. Thank you, Leila."

She looked down and saw that Roscoe was on his side, breathing rapidly. "What did you do to Roscoe?"

"I kicked him. Now just give me what I want and I won't bother you again."

"You lie. You'll kill us all," Leila said calmly.

Vugar smiled. "Maybe," he agreed. "Guards, seize their weapons," Vugar demanded.

Two guys dressed in black grabbed both of their guns and Linc's knife, but not Leila's.

"Come out from hiding behind your girlfriend, Mr. Hart."

Linc didn't. Instead, he grabbed the knife from the sheath at Leila's waist.

"The boss said to quit hiding," one of the guards said as he pushed Linc next to Leila.

"Keep your hands off him," Leila said sharply. "I'll tell you everything I know, which includes where the nukes are coming from. That way you can bypass the middleman."

Linc saw Vugar's eyes gleam.

"How soon can I get them?"

"According to what I've learned, you could probably have them in your hands next week." Leila shrugged. "Let everybody else go. It's me you want."

"They're my leverage that you will tell me the truth."

"The man behind me is your leverage. I love him. Let the Murphys go." Linc watched Vugar considering it.

"They're just going to be an inconvenience," she prompted.

"I could kill them now," Vugar said.

"Like you did your brother? Look what a bind that got you in. I'm pretty stubborn, if you remember. You kill my friends and you'll never get the information you want from me."

"Better yet. You come with me. I have a helicopter landing soon, and we can all take a little trip. Your neighbors and their dog can stay here."

Leila nodded. "Can I ask a question?"

"You can ask. That doesn't mean I'm going to answer it."

"Why now? Why do you need to put your hands on the nukes now, five months later?"

"I have a buyer who is insistent I provide what my little brother advertised. He has been very persuasive that I get him what he wants."

Linc tried to assimilate what Vugar was saying. This man practically had a personal army at his beck and call. Why not just tell this buyer to fuck off?

"He's threatening you," Leila surmised.

Vugar nodded. "But I'll soon stop that from happening. It's just a matter of time."

"He's fucking with your deliveries, isn't he? Probably your procurement, too," Linc guessed.

"What do you know about that?"

"Who's your customer?" Leila asked indifferently.

Vugar shrugged his shoulders.

"What country?" Linc asked.

Leila watched Vugar's expression turn smug.

Fuck, he wasn't selling to a country; he was selling to an individual or a consortium!

"Your customer, he's threatening to burn your house down, isn't he? Wipe out all your tech, all your accounts, turn you into nothing if you don't give him what he wants," Leila taunted him.

Vugar turned ashen.

They were all in trouble if individuals now wanted nuclear capabilities.

Come on, Leila, get him to tell you who the buyer is.

"I'm curious. Who's more powerful than you?" Leila taunted further.

When they heard the *whomp-whomp* of the helicopter coming, Jase wanted to blast Vugar to hell, but Leila grasped his hand, holding tight. She was reminding him they had to stay the course.

"R.L. Bonner is my customer. But he isn't more powerful than me." Vugar said as they got close to the helicopter. "Now I left your friends alive. I expect my return information." He said with a bite.

Vugar stepped onto the helicopter first. Then one guard grabbed Linc and another grabbed Leila to push them into the helicopter.

Linc easily elbowed his guard in the face, then kicked him in the side of his kneecap and watched him go down in agony. Leila had done an impressive twist and punched her guard in the throat.

Vugar was looking at them both with fury. He held onto one rail as he reached out trying to catch Leila's arm as the helicopter started to lift off.

It was enough. Linc threw the knife and it went straight through Vugar's eye. His good eye stayed open for a moment and looked at Linc in amazement, then Linc watched with pleasure as the life drained out of him.

EPILOGUE

When Leila had enlisted the help of the women of Omega Sky, she had no idea just how out-of-control things would become. Lincoln was turning thirty, and Leila wanted to celebrate this day, this year, and this man. She'd heard more stories from Linc over the months they'd lived together. For some reason his biological dad would never allow his mother to celebrate Linc's birthdays. The one time she'd baked Linc a cake, his father had pushed her face into it before he started to hit her. Connie Hart tried to make up for it after she married George, but times were lean in the beginning, so Linc told her to save the money for the younger kids.

He deserved an exceptional birthday party.

She'd called his mom and told her what she had in mind. And Connie got the Minnesota contingent assembled. The ladies got the SEAL team rounded up, and volunteered Gideon's house for the party because it was a showplace. Leila said she would take care of catering and decorations.

But then she had a translation gig that was too lucrative to pass up. By the time she got back, Lark, Jada, and Amy had figured out the catering and the decorations, and it was all awesome. Almost everybody who wasn't local was staying at the same hotel. She suggested that even the local folk park their cars at the hotel, and she would arrange a bus to drive them to the party so Linc wouldn't be tipped off with all the cars near Gideon's house.

She had told Linc that she wouldn't be home until two days after his birthday, but that she had made reservations at a new restaurant in town where they could celebrate. He said that would be great. Since she actually got home a day earlier, she checked into the same hotel as everybody else, then she went shopping for a knockout dress with her mom. She intended this birthday to be memorable.

LINC COULDN'T WAIT for Leila to come home. He had something really special for her. Two days from now was the second anniversary of when they first met in Turkey and he wanted to surprise her. And he was pretty sure he had it nailed.

She was supposed to be home tomorrow and that was when they were going to celebrate his birthday and then the day after, his surprise. He wanted to show Jase and Gideon today and let them poke any holes in it. See if he should change how to tell her. Having Gideon invite them over to watch the game and do some barbeque was perfect. He took the legal-size manilla envelope with him as he started up the pathway to Gideon's front door.

Maybe a little tug-o-war with Gideon's horse of a dog

named Lucy would be fun, too. He'd never talked about animals with Leila, but he'd like to get a dog. Yeah, he couldn't wait for forty-eight hours from now.

He knocked on Gideon's door.

"Come in," Gideon yelled.

He walked into the hallway and stopped short as a crowd of people yelled out, *Happy Birthday.*

Then up walked Leila in a pair of red fuck-me shoes and a red dress that molded to her body. He thought his head might explode.

Behind Leila were his mom and dad and Leila's mom and dad. Then behind them were all of his brothers and sisters.

What the hell?

"I can't believe this," he whispered as he hugged Leila. "How is this even possible?"

"The big three-oh is momentous. Many people wanted to be here to celebrate."

"Hiya, Uncle Lincoln. I drewed up pictures for you." His niece Georgia smiled up at him.

"This is beautiful. What is it?"

"A fairy."

He looked at the three purple circles. "Ahhh."

He picked her up and nuzzled the baby fat of her neck. Holding her high in his arms, he turned to his mom and dad.

"Thank you so much for making the trip." His dad plucked his namesake out of Linc's arms so he could give his mother a proper hug.

"We wouldn't have missed this for the world. I love your girl is making a big deal of this. I think the world of her."

"So do I, Mom."

"Well, you better do something about it before you're too old and decrepit." She kissed him on the cheek and passed him over to his dad.

"You're looking pretty happy, Son."

"I am."

"Couldn't ask for more."

"When things die down a bit, can I pull you and a couple of my friends aside? I want to get your take on something."

"You've got it." That was his dad. He always had his six.

He made sure that he took time to talk to Miray and Grant. He really liked them, so it wasn't a hardship. But it was always good to keep the wheels greased with your woman's family. Before he went to talk to his brothers and sisters, he went into Gideon's office and put the manilla envelope on the top shelf of his bookcase.

It was a beautiful day, so most of the party was outside. There was a mountain of food and a volleyball net was set up and so was a croquet set. It wasn't until dusk that the toasts to him started. He thanked God that most of them poked fun and were humorous.

But when his dad spoke and told everyone that he couldn't have been prouder of the man Linc had turned into, there was hardly a dry eye in the house.

Last, it was Leila's turn.

"To Lincoln Hart. I'll love you until forever ends."

Aw, shit. Now I'm going to cry.

He got up and took her into his arms and pressed his lips to hers. It was both a prayer and a promise. When he was done and they were both breathless, he turned to the room filled with his family and friends.

"Hey, Gideon, I stuck a manilla envelope on top of

your bookcase in your office when I got here today. Can you bring it to me?"

Gideon lifted his chin and brought it to him in less than a minute.

Linc turned to Leila. "Okay, baby, I'm not sure which should come first. And don't think I'm dictating to you. This is me trying to make our joint dreams come true. But I can always scrub the mission."

There were a lot of masculine chuckles in the room.

Linc pulled out a sheaf of papers. It showed the house that they had been drooling over for the last four months. It had never come on the market, but he'd found a real estate agent who felt comfortable asking if the homeowners would be willing to sell. They were.

Linc negotiated an offer that was in his and Leila's agreed upon price range, and he put down earnest money that could be retracted within five days without penalty.

He watched Leila skim through the document.

"How did you manage to do this? Your superpowers?"

He nodded his head. "Do you like it?"

"I love it."

"But there is one stipulation."

Leila frowned. "I didn't see one in the papers."

He dug into the manilla envelope again, and this time he came out with a blue box. "I want to live in this house as a married couple. You have always been my destiny, and I want to build a life together. Will you marry me?"

He thumbed open the box and she gasped. It was a square-cut orange sapphire with a square diamond on each side.

She said nothing. After looking at the ring, she just stared up at his face.

"Leila," he prompted gently. "Don't leave me hanging."

She gave him a slow smile. "You're right. We were destined to be together. Of course, I'll marry you."

Coming up is Her Defiant Warrior, Book Five. Grab your copy now!

ABOUT THE AUTHOR

Caitlyn O'Leary is a USA Bestselling Author, #1 Amazon Bestselling Author and a Golden Quill Recipient from Book Viral in 2015. Hampered with a mild form of dyslexia she began memorizing books at an early age until her grandmother, the English teacher, took the time to teach her to read -- then she never stopped. She began re-writing alternate endings for her Trixie Belden books into happily-ever-afters with Trixie's platonic friend Jim. When she was home with pneumonia at twelve, she read the entire set of World Book Encyclopedias -- a little more challenging to end those happily.

Caitlyn loves writing about Alpha males with strong heroines who keep the men on their toes. There is plenty of action, suspense and humor in her books. She is never shy about tackling some of today's tough and relevant issues.

In addition to being an award-winning author of romantic suspense novels, she is a devoted aunt, an avid reader, a former corporate executive for a Fortune 100 company, and totally in love with her husband of soon-to-be twenty years.

She recently moved back home to the Pacific Northwest from Southern California. She is so happy to see the seasons again; rain, rain and more rain. She has a large fan group on Facebook and through her e-mail list. Caitlyn is known for telling her "Caitlyn Factors", where she relates her little and big life's screw-ups. The list is long. She loves hearing and connecting with her fans on a daily basis.

Keep up with Caitlyn O'Leary:

Website: www.caitlynoleary.com
FB Reader Group: http://bit.ly/2NUZVjF
Email: caitlyn@caitlynoleary.com
Newsletter: http://bit.ly/1WIhRup

facebook.com/Caitlyn-OLeary-Author-638771522866740
twitter.com/CaitlynOLearyNA
instagram.com/caitlynoleary_author
amazon.com/author/caitlynoleary
bookbub.com/authors/caitlyn-o-leary
goodreads.com/CaitlynOLeary
pinterest.com/caitlynoleary35

ALSO BY CAITLYN O'LEARY

Her Steadfast Hero (Book #1)

Her Devoted Hero (Book #2)

Her Passionate Hero (Book #3)

Her Wicked Hero (Book #4)

Her Guarded Hero (Book #5)

Her Captivated Hero (Book #6)

Her Honorable Hero (Book #7)

Her Loving Hero (Book #8)

THE MIDNIGHT DELTA SERIES

Her Vigilant Seal (Book #1)

Her Loyal Seal (Book #2)

Her Adoring Seal (Book #3)

Sealed with a Kiss (Book #4)

Her Daring Seal (Book #5)

Her Fierce Seal (Book #6)

A Seals Vigilant Heart (Book #7)

Her Dominant Seal (Book #8)

Her Relentless Seal (Book #9)

Her Treasured Seal (Book #10)

Her Unbroken Seal (Book #11)

THE LONG ROAD HOME

Defending Home

Home Again

FATE HARBOR

Trusting Chance

Protecting Olivia

Isabella's Submission

Claiming Kara

Cherishing Brianna

<u>Silver SEALs</u>

Seal At Sunrise

<u>Shadows Alliance Series</u>

Declan

Made in the USA
Coppell, TX
08 August 2023

20134254R00157